C072108

DISCARD

P9-DCP-078

D C

H. MP.

KING OF SILVERHILL

Bad luck seems to dog King Coleman and his partner, Em Moon. A dry spell finishes their ranching business while a gold claim yields more hope than gold. So they pull up stakes and head for the Clockman Mines to find work.

On the way, King risks his life to rescue a girl from a treacherous cliff. Vicki Marlow tells him she is a photographer for an Eastern newspaper, assigned to report on the Clockman Mines. They travel there together, only to find that the mines are run so badly that there must be sabotage in the air . . .

KING OF
SILVERHILL

Archie Joscelyn

WESTERNS

First published 1964
by Arcadia House

This hardback edition 1992
by Chivers Press
by arrangement with
Donald MacCampbell Inc.

ISBN 0 7451 4534 5

Copyright 1964, by Arcadia House

British Library Cataloguing in Publication Data available

Printed and bound in Great Britain by
Redwood Press Limited, Melksham, Wiltshire

KING OF SILVERHILL

1.

"Old Woman must have spilled her bucket of mop water—and it shows plenty muddy," Coleman observed to himself. "It's sure comin' down like Lake Tahoe had got above us and sprung a leak. Rain, where were you where I used to be?"

He lifted his face to the pelting drive of storm, with an outdoor man's enjoyment of weather. Until today, it had been much too long since there had been any rain to be out in, and he was there for the lack of it, just as Emory Moon, riding the last of the ten wagons in line, was there for the lack of it. But that was life. It rained or there was drought, and you took the bad with the good, the dry with the wet.

This was supposed to be dry season in the Washoes. Instead, the rain spilled endlessly from clouds which hovered over the shivering earth like a hen too solicitous for her chicks, and the wagons slipped and slid over increasingly rough trails dignified by the name of roads. An hour before, they'd come through Rock Camp, a collection of shacks huddled close against a squashed cake of a hill. The cabins reminded Coleman of toadstools a day past their prime, rank with decay. Masked by storm, their appearance had suggested not riches but poverty. Well, *borrasco*—hard times— was across the land. Even in the silver hills its curse had not been exorcised.

Coleman has noticed the sign on one shed-like building at the edge of the town: H. VAN CLEEVE, Assay Office. There, at least, prosperity should perch, since this was mining country. But the outward appearance gave no indication of it.

Another hour should bring them to Silverhill. There the miners who burrowed mole-like near the mountain top lived, as did the teamsters who hauled the ore, and all the others who in one way or another gained livelihood from the mining camp. Helltop reared beyond—the hill of silver, a place of trouble and danger.

Coleman's eight horses, animals of bone and brawn who were no more than distant cousins to the cayuse, edged around a jackknife bend in the road. One of the leaders snorted, puffing windily through its nostrils. A voice called faintly: "Help!"

Coleman, huddled on the wet seat, had had the appearance of a sleepy bear. The drowsy air was deceptive. He was instantly alert, acting instinctively even as his eyes swept the steep slope of hillside above and below the road. He called, "Whoa," and kicked the brake down hard, reaching as part of the same gesture to wrap the reins around its handle, leaving himself free to act.

A saddled horse stood a score of feet below the road, where the steeply descending hill widened temporarily to a sort of shelf. The cayuse shivered on three legs, with one foreleg dangling.

The saddle had been shoved crazily to the side and back, though the cinch still held. The right hip of the pony was gashed and muddy. There was a companion scratch down the hill below the road. The cayuse had lost its footing, then plunged and slid before managing to come to a halt, one foreleg broken.

There was no sign of the rider, but on below the pitch continued very steep. Then it ended at a precipice. What had happened was clear. The rider had been thrown as the horse fell, and had gone down and over.

Coleman jumped, not bothering with the hub of the big front wheel as he usually did in descending. Panic and desperation had throbbed in that cry for help. His team, he hoped, would stand; he'd risk that. For Mike Flood, driving the next wagon in line, would be coming up to see what was wrong.

Coleman was running as his feet hit the road, following it past the horses, mud splashing with each step. There was room for him, but none to spare. These mountain roads, dug out of the side of the hill, had to be wide enough for one vehicle, with an occasional spot where two wagons might pass.

After a dozen strides, Coleman left the road, keeping a precarious footing on the slope below. The grass was like oil, adding to the hazard of the mud, but Coleman had ever been kin to a goat when it came to hills. He did not slacken pace or break stride.

Now, below the saddled horse, he could see past the rim of cliff. The rain made a gray haze of the valley farther down, with distant treetops and a tiny thread of creek showing. Then he saw the rider, and shock rippled through him. The distressed horseman was a woman.

Slipping over the brink, she had sought to save herself, clutching at a handhold, securing it on the branches of a shrub which grew at the cliff's edge. But such a hold was insecure at best. The handful of slender branches had bent, allowing her to go over. Now, stretched to their full length of four or five feet, the branches hung straight down, and the girl, hands clasping them desperately, clung wth feet dangling in the air.

In the tumble, her hat had been lost, allowing her

hair to spill about her face and shoulders. It reached
to her waist, as richly yellow as the gold which old
Zeb Clockman had once vainly hunted among these
hills.

The shrub was tough and resilient, as befitted any
living thing which could survive in so bleakly exposed
a position, and so far the shoots had endured the severe
strain put upon them. But the root was giving trouble.
The bush had obtained a precarious roothold to begin
with. Now its roots were tearing loose, popping from
thin gravelly earth. They would give way at any
moment.

Coleman saw that and knew a moment of panic.
The face uplifted to his was rain-washed, but young
and with a beauty to match the wealth of her hair.
Wide blue eyes met his in agonized appeal.

What was to be done had to be done swiftly. The
roots were tearing loose before his eyes. But nature
had provided a chance of sorts.

Below the bush, the cliff ran in either direction, as
neatly as though the wall had been laid by a stone-
mason. The wall descended straight for half a hundred
feet, before the slope of hill again took charge. But the
prankish mason had left one stone which jutted out
below, at the side where the girl hung. It was like a
perch, a couple of feet long and about half as wide.

On the far side from the girl and slightly lower

down, the wall widened to a small shelf. Again, it was no more than a yard in width or length. The hitch was that both these possible places of succor were out of reach of her dangling feet.

"Tailor-made for Ol' King Cole," Coleman muttered, and jumped.

His feet hit the perch, knees bending to absorb part of the shock following a ten-foot drop. The rock had been worn and polished by rain and wind and sun over the centuries, and it was almost as slippery as the mud and grass above. But the fortunate part was that it was anchored solidly. It did not break or tear loose beneath him.

The effect was precisely what Coleman had hoped. He bounced like a ball, launching forward, and all he had to do was open his arms and clasp, and the girl was in them. Pellets of mud and gravel rained upon him as the roots continued to give way. It wasn't necessary for the girl to let go as he grabbed. Her support was taking care of that.

The impetus of his jump carried Coleman the next half-dozen feet, and the fact that the shelf was a bit lower made it all right. He hit and flung his body toward the hill, straining hard for balance. There was room enough, but none to spare, and if they kept on sliding, the prospect below offered scant encouragement.

One boot was holding, his other sliding outward. Coleman brought it closer, hitting down hard with the hob nails, feeling them grip. They stood, his arms about her, locked in close embrace, and he felt the tenseness of her body, then the relaxation as she sensed that they had come to a full stop. But she did not make the mistake of trying to move or disengage herself.

Coleman let out his breath, then drew it in again. There had been no time for thinking or considering, only for action. Luck had been with him—luck with a big L. Suddenly the girl was trembling, and he realized the desperate strain she had been under. His clasp tightened protectively.

"Nothing to worry about now," he said reassuringly, and was surprised at the huskiness of his voice. "There's help at hand. Get a rope, Mike," he added, in a shout. "Down here."

"Right with you, King!" Flood's voice came like a bellow. "Where the blazes are you?"

"Down here, perched on the side of the cliff like nestin' swallows. Take your time, but don't waste ours."

Back at the ranch, Coleman had acted as his own foreman, and Mike Flood had been his right-hand man, always cool, swiftly competent in an emergency. He could read sign as well as Coleman had done, and Mike had a rope on his wagon.

It was difficult to keep their perch and look nearly straight up to where Flood was. But the end of the rope came down and rasped past King's ear. Coleman felt better as his fingers closed around it.

"Get some of the boys to help you, Mike," he instructed. "Then pull the lady up—and be gentle about it."

Moving carefully, he adjusted the noose around the girl and under her arms.

"You ready?" Moon rolled down.

"Ready and willing," Coleman assured him.

The girl reached to set red and blistered hands on the rope and hold fast; then she was lifted smoothly. Presently the rope came down again, and, not bothering with the air lift, Coleman climbed it to stand beside his crew. All were wet as the proverbial rat, but cheerful and excited. Color was returning to the girl's white face, and she smiled tremulously as he joined them.

"I can't ever thank you enough—all of you, but you especially. I couldn't have held on any longer—and the bush was tearing loose." She closed her eyes tightly as though to shut out the memory, opened them again. "I never was so glad to meet anybody in my life," she ended with a gallant attempt at lightness.

"It was mutual, ma'am," Coleman told her.

"I'm Lynn Coleman," he added. "This is Emory Moon, my partner—and our boys; the list is too long to introduce till we have a better chance. Here on this hill, they'd paw and scrape and likely start a slide again."

"We sure hope you ain't took no hurt, ma'am," Moon said. "That was a mighty chancy happenin'."

"I'm fine, Mr. Moon, thanks to all of you," she returned. "I'm Vicki Marlow—out here to take pictures of the mines and write a piece for an eastern paper." She lifted anxious eyes to where her horse stood, and Coleman saw her lower lip catch painfully between her teeth. "I'm afraid my poor beast has broken its leg. What—is there anything we can do?"

"Best thing will be to put the poor critter out of its misery, I guess," Coleman said. "How did it happen?"

"I hardly know. Something frightened him very suddenly. I couldn't see anything, but all at once he spun about and pitched without warning. He lost his footing and went over the edge of the road—"

"How long ago?" Moon demanded, and waved a hand at the others. "Get back to your teams, boys!" Coleman understood his apprehension. What she had said sounded as though the cayuse might have caught a whiff of bear or puma. If the same animal should still be lurking in the vicinity, it would be bad if the eight-horse teams boogered.

"I suppose it was a quarter of an hour or so. I fell and slid, then managed to grab that bush. I held fast, and it seemed like an eternity before I heard your wagon. But actually it couldn't have been very long."

"You headin' for Silverhill?" Coleman asked. "If that's it, you can ride with us. Mike will put your horse out of its misery after we go on. It's the only way," he added gently.

"I suppose so," she agreed. "But careful of the pack, please. I hope my camera isn't smashed."

Dan O'Leary, his red face matching his hair, was already pulling off saddle and pack. He carried it up the slope and deposited it on Coleman's wagon, then turned resignedly.

"I suppose so," she agreed. "Be careful of the pack, wistfully.

"She sure will—'less she prefers Moon's society." Coleman grinned. "We better get going, if we're to reach town before dark." He lifted her up over the wheel, took his place and kicked loose the brake. The wagons ground into motion, and nothing was said until presently there sounded the muffled report of a rifle. Once more, the girl was biting an already red lip. There were tears on her face now, not to be confused with the rain.

"The poor critter's troubles are over," Coleman said gently. "Lucky it ended up no worse."

"As it would have, but for you," she said, and turned quickly." You were wonderful, Mr. Coleman—there wasn't a moment to spare, and you didn't waste any. I can never thank you enough."

"That's all over with," he said uncomfortably. "And I'm not Mister. My friends call me King."

"King Coleman!" she breathed, and a smile softened the edges of her mouth. "I think it's a fitting title!"

"Why, no, just natural, because of that old rhyme," he protested. "My name's Lynn, and it was pretty easy to twist it."

She glanced back at the line of big wagons strung out in the rain.

"Are these your wagons, Mr.—King?"

"Well—more or less. Em Moon and I are partners. We're headin' for Silverhill in the hope of getting a job hauling ore. Sort of staving off the wolf, as you might put it."

She frowned, clearly at a loss. Even when she frowned she was mighty pretty, King decided.

"I'm afraid I don't quite understand—"

"Well, it's like this," King explained. "Em Moon and I have been more or less partners, off and on, for the last score of years. That partnership business comes mainly out of the goodness of Moon's heart, of course. I was orphaned when I was a little shaver, and for a spell, things were rough. Way I met Moon, I was tryin' to ride a hammer-headed cayuse, and I got piled. I wasn't hardly big enough to straddle the saddle, or with long enough legs to stretch and tuck my toes in the stirrup leathers. Anyway, my head was whirling when Moon picked me up."

"You poor little fellow!" Her face was soft with sympathy.

"That was a lucky break—for me. Moon looked after me. Mostly it's been a one-way road, with Moon giving most of the assists. A while back, we were doing pretty good. Seemed to us like we'd struck a bonanza—money to jingle. I'd always wanted a ranch, and I got hold of a nice little spread out from Stockton—in California. Moon, he never could see himself lookin' at the tail end of a cow, but with a horse built like an elephant it was different. He wanted to have big wagons, loaded with freight, to carry goods to settlers in a growing country. So he got that, too, off south from where I was. And for a couple of years we figured we'd made it."

"But something went wrong?"

"Bonanza turned out to be *borrasco*—which it has pretty much over the whole country, as far as that goes." Seeing her bewilderment, he explained, *"Borrasco's* Spanish, same as bonanza—meanin' about the opposite. Another word for hard times."

Vicki nodded. "There are plenty of those everywhere," she agreed.

"There sure are. Now with me, I thought I was settin' pretty, but all at once I discovered I was cattle

poor. I've got a good spread, and for a while we had
rain enough to get by. Then it got dry, and the grass
dried up. Cattle close to starvin', so I had to sell some.
But when the meat on a steer is worth less than his hide,
and that's not worth the effort it takes to peel it from
the carcass—well, it was *borrasco*."

"And Moon?"

"With Moon it was a drying up of business, same as
the ground turning from mud to dust, and the grass
from green to brown under a burnin' sun. Folks can't
buy much stuff when they've no money. So his business dried up along with the rest. Then he turned his
teams out to pasture, where they'd been fine for a couple
of years. But the grass was turnin' short, and the horses
hunted out loco weed, which they'd neglected when feed
was lush. By the time Moon discovered it, they were
sure loco, and he near went the same."

"You poor men!"

"Poor, nothing!" King snorted. "Just broke, is all—
and there's a difference. But I got to lookin' around and
heard about the silver mines here. So I put it up to
Moon.

" 'You've still got your wagons, Em,' I told him. 'And
I have the horses to pull them.' I wrote to Bart Apperson, who's general foreman for the Clockman Mines,
and asked him what were the chances of hauling ore—
we had the wagons, teams, men. His answer was

middlin' encouragin'. He said that was a good combination, though there was no work for men alone, or
wagons or horses alone. But there was lots of hauling
to be done, and if I wanted to risk it, there might be
work when we got here."

"But you're not sure?"

"Almost. There'd be work, he said, providing we
arrived ahead of others who might get the same notion.
'Course, if too many came, there might not be work for
all, and those first on the scene would get the job."

"So you're gambling?"

"Well, you could call it that—though with nothing
behind us, it's not too big a gamble. We've been ten
days on the road, and we'll soon know."

"And if you get the job, you'll be all right?"

"Finer'n frog hair. It'll keep us eatin'. Moon did a
lot of figurin'. He knows hauling, which I don't. The
wages aren't much, even for a silver camp. On the other
hand, they're fair for times like these. Two dollars a
day for a wagon, five dollars for eight horses, three
dollars for a man. That's ten dollars a wagon and what's
needed to keep it rollin'."

"It doesn't seem like much."

"It's scratchin' small, Moon decided. We sure won't
get fat. On the other hand, hay is cheap these days,
and board not too bad. We can live and pay our boys
and maybe make a couple of bucks a day per outfit.

A hundred a week, with luck."

"And later you hope to go back to your ranch, and Moon to his freighting business?"

"A man has to have something to dream about." King grinned. "That's what keeps you going when things get rough."

"So you'll actually be working for the Clockman Mines! I understand that they are quite a big operation."

"I guess they are," King agreed, "though I've heard rumors that they aren't turnin' out to be the bonanza they were expected to be. Old Zeb Clockman spent most of his life searching for gold. He tramped the deserts and climbed the mountains. I've seen these old desert rats, sniffin' hopeful as a hungry coyote, and scratchin' as frustrated as that same varmint above a holed-up gopher. It's one thing to know that the gopher is down there somewhere. But locating it and getting it out is something else."

"But Zeb Clockman made his strike!"

"Yeah—more or less. He spent his life hunting for gold, then had to settle for silver. And he found that on top of one of the highest, wildest, most unfriendly peaks in the whole Washoe range. But I guess he was satisfied."

A small stream burbled close beside the road, dropping fast in a series of waterfalls and cascades. The road

made a sharp angle and climbed steeply, sloping outward to where brush cloaked a canyon. Wheel tracks
showed where some vehicles had come close to sliding
off.

Reaching the crest, Coleman allowed the horse to
stand and blow. The rain-shrouded valley was rough
and gloomy—a wild, remote country which man was
feebly attempting to tame and harness to his own ends.
King went on cheerfully:

"Somehow, Zeb scraped up capital and made a start.
Times weren't quite so bad then, the silver was bonanza,
a magic word. Zeb got a road built up the mountain—
they say it's a lollapalooza, a climbing trail to the sky.
Wagons crawl up there and haul ore down, then across
country about a three-day journey to the smelter. It
was supposed to be fabulous, that ore, but I guess such
reports were over-optimistic. The operation's still going,
but a lot of the glitter has faded."

"That's life, isn't it?"

"It sure is. And now old Zeb is dead, and they say he
has a son back East who's living high on the hog from
what the mines produce, and who shuns his daddy's
waverin' footsteps and chooses not to walk therein.
Maybe he's smart. There's been a lot of trouble con-
nected with that strike. The hill's got itself a new name
the last couple of years—Helltop."

He squinted ahead through the storm and thickening

gloom. Yellow lights were beginning to show, swimming in a misty pool of darkness.

"Looks like we're coming to Silverhill," he commented, "which will give us a chance to get in out of the wet." He considered her anxiously. "You got any place in mind to stay?"

"Why, no." Vicki's reply was puzzled. "I expected to go to the hotel."

"We'll try it, then, and hope for the best."

"What do you mean?"

"*Borrasco* everywhere," he explained. "Hard times puts lots of people out of work. So they flock to such places as Silverhill, where they hope there's at least a chance of a job. Which makes for crowded conditions."

She considered that while they came to the town. Not much could be seen in the storm and gathering dusk. Here and there the lights revealed the street as a churned-up stretch of mud and water. The whole was unlovely and far from homelike, at least according to her notions. By day it would probably look even worse. But it was her destination, the girl reminded herself, and she'd make the best of it.

"You mean there may not be any rooms at the hotel?"

King grinned again.

"Now I've made you fret," he chided himself. "If there's no room, we'll sure enough find one somewhere."

"But you—don't you and your men have some place in mind?"

"We can sleep under the wagons, or in a barn, if we have to. Here's the hotel, looks like. Nothin' like findin' out."

The hotel, of unpainted clapboards, two stories tall, loomed at the side. The sign said: PALACE HOTEL. Three steps led up to the porch. Turning the noses of his horses in at the hitch rail, King jumped down, reached to assist Vicki, and led the way inside.

Two coal-oil lamps lighted the nearly bare lobby, where several men lounged near the pot-bellied heater which glowed warmly in the middle of the room. The clerk, behind the desk, had apparently just entered from the storm. He still wore a hat and coat, and he looked up as they entered, stared a moment, then called out.

"Folks, you're lucky!" he declared. "I reckon you want a room on this wet and miserable night, and by gorry, I've got just one room. Feller that had it, uh—met with an accident."

Vicki glanced questioningly about, then, as a couple of the men moved back politely from the stove, held chilled hands toward it. Color flooded her cheeks as the clerk rushed on.

"Sure makes it lucky for you, me havin' a vacancy. I reckon you're man and wife, so that'll make it fine."

2.

Vicki pivoted like a cutting horse, her lips parting, but she did not speak; only looked at Coleman. His own face was red, but his disarming grin made light of the error.

"Seems like you're takin' a long runnin' jump at conclusions, friend. It's the lady who wants the room. Her horse fell with her a few miles back. Broke its leg. I gave her a ride on into town."

There was an embarrassed moment while the clerk fumbled with a heavy sweep of mustache. He gazed with rapt attention at a cockroach which ventured from under the corner of the desk, then scuttled back.

"Uh—I'm right sorry for bein' hasty," he apologized. "Seems like I have a capacity for openin' my mouth and findin' my foot in it. You folks ain't married, then?"

"No," King agreed. "An hour's acquaintance is a little short. But Miss Marlow needs a room, the best you've got."

Slowly, regretfully, the clerk shook his head.

"I wouldn't be disputin' that none," he conceded. "And I'm mighty sorry. If you folks just happened to be married, I reckon it'd be all right. But everybody else in this hotel is a man. So I'm afraid it just wouldn't do."

Color was higher in Vicki's cheeks, and King recognized the unanswerable logic of the decision. "We'll find some place for you to stay," he promised, and silence hung heavily over the room as they turned back to the door.

Moon was waiting beside King's wagon as they came out. His cavalry type mustache was frayed and drooping, but he swept off his hat with a gallantry which took no account of the brimfull of rainwater which the action splashed across his face.

"I trust you ain't feelin' no ill effects from your experience, Miss Vicki, ma'am" he said. "Seems like you're gettin' an over-wet baptism into the life of the West, for which we're plumb regretful."

Vicki managed a twisted smile. Despite herself, her lip trembled.

King stepped quckly into the breach.

"The hotel's full up," he said. "We've got to find a good place for her to stay. There have to be such places."

"Crowded, eh?" Moons tone was reflective rather than

surprised. "Then we'll sure find one. I noticed there's a boarding house right across the street. Let's see can we get something to eat, and maybe we can find out somethin' there. You boys take the teams on down to the stable, then come back," he added.

Darkness now covered the town, made more opaque by the steady pelting of rain, but the unmistakable odor of a livery barn came warmly from farther down the street. There would at least be fodder and shelter for the teams.

The street was a lane of mud and water, deep-rutted by the ore wagons. Moon resettled his hat and led the way.

"Excuse me," King said, and swept Vicki up into his arms, then followed. "Save you from getting bogged down," he added, and deposited her on the plank walk opposite. A wider street, he reflected, would have been nice.

Moon pushed open the door. Inside were warmth and light and the savory temptation of food. A long table with a red and white checked tablecloth was laden with it, but every chair around the table was occupied. A tall girl, with hair like old ivory piled in a bun atop her head, came in with a steaming platter. Moon accosted her respectfully.

"Excuse me, ma'am," he said. "But we saw the sign— and we'd sure like to get some supper. There's 'leven of us, all told, and we're mighty sharp set—"

The girl was staring stolidly at him as though she did not hear. One of the boarders swung about to look at them. His glance quickened with approval at sight of Vicki, turned disdainful as it rested on Moon.

"This place is full up," he said. "It's a boarding house; not a restaurant."

"You run it, maybe?" Moon asked mildly. "You're the landlord?"

"Naw, I just eat here. But like you can see—"

"That's what we want to do, too—eat. When I talk, I always like to talk to the boss." Moon turned back to the girl. "Like I say, we're wet and hungry—"

The boarder interrupted again. "Lena's new over from the old country. She don't savvy much English."

A voice sounded from the adjoining kitchen.

"It's like Mr. DeQuille was saying: we can't take any extras. 'Course, I'm sorry, but—"

The speaker came through the doorway, bearing a bowl, as the girl darted back to the kitchen's haven. The landlady was a small, neat woman, surprisingly pretty. She stopped abruptly, staring at Moon. His eyes were popping in turn.

For a moment there was no sound, and even the hungry diners looked up, sensing something out of the ordinary. The landlady's face was the hue of flour, and her hands shook so that the bowl threatened to drop.

King stepped hastily forward and caught it. She did not even notice him.

"Emory Moon!" she gasped. "It is you, Em!"

Moon's sharp, usually dour face was expanding with delight.

"Sure it's me," he agreed. "Couldn't be anybody else. And it's you, Maggie—Maggie Smith!"

Color came back to her face, chasing the ghost of a smile.

"Not Maggie Smith for many a year, Emory. Maggie Travis."

"Sure now, of course." The glow of delight faded from Moon's eyes. "It sort of slipped my mind, in the pleasure of seein' you again. Uh—how is Tom, the durned old reprobate?"

For the first time, Mrs. Travis seemed to take note of King and the bowl which he held. It was apparent that she welcomed the chance to compose her thoughts.

"You can set those spuds on the table, for those starving creatures," she suggested. "And thank you kindly. Tom," she added, "has been in his grave these ten years, Emory."

The light came back into Moon's face as though a candle had been lit within a jack-o'-lantern.

"Now that's the best news I've heard in years," he blurted. 'But I'm ready and willing, as always, to take his place—" He stopped, pink to the tips of his mustache.

"Er—I'm sorry, Maggie. I didn't mean that just the way it sounded—"

Both looked around the room as though suddenly remembering the others. Maggie Travis became brisk.

"I know, Emory," she agreed. "This is so sudden that it kind of catches one between wind and water. To think of findin' you here! But I mind you were sayin' that you and your friends were hungry. 'Course, men always are. But come on and bring them in. What are you waiting for? I'll find something for you to eat, for old times' sake."

As the regulars finished, she shooed them out, so that the table could be reset for the newcomers. Moon introduced Vicki.

"This lady is just in from the East, Maggie. She writes for a newspaper or something. Her horse broke a leg back a few miles, and she got a bad tumble. Rode on in with us. Now the hotel's full up, and there's no place for her to stay—"

"You poor dear," Maggie sympathized. "You couldn't stay at that hotel if there was room. I'll find you a place right here. Though as for you, Moon, and the rest of your boys—eleven, did you say—"

"There's King Coleman here, and myself, and eight of our crew," Moon explained. "But don't worry about us. If we can get something to eat, we'll make out."

"It'll mean an extra table, but you can board here if

you can stand my cooking," Maggie agreed. "That much I can do for old times' sake, Em."

"I could eat your cookin' three times a day and relish it," Moon declared gallantly, "as I've liked to do all these years!"

The others returned, reporting the teams were cared for. The men could sleep in the barn overnight, while the rain continued. Lena came back from the kitchen, carrying a fresh platter, and colored at the look which Dan O'Leary bent on her. To everyone's surprise, he said a few words in what appeared to be her native tongue. Lena stared a moment, then, her face lighting with pleasure, broke into a torrent of speech. O'Leary held up a big hand.

"Whoa, now, take it easy," he adjured. "I can talk a few words if you go slow—" He shifted from English, and apparently made himself understood. Flood eyed him curiously as Lena returned to the kitchen.

"I thought all you spoke was English, you big Irishman, and not much of that," he protested. "Where'd you learn Skowhegan?"

"That's Danish," O'Leary retorted. "We used to have a neighbor when I was a kid—liked his Copenhagen 'cause that's where he was from. Taught me to like it, too, along with fishin', and a few of the words. Poor kid's sort of homesick," he added pensively.

"She must be," Flood agreed, and winked at King.

When they were fed and warmed, the prospects were more encouraging. It had been a stroke of luck, Moon meeting the only girl he had ever courted. King had known, without mention being made of the subject, that it was her memory which had kept Moon from ever looking twice at any other woman. Now, if their luck would hold—

There was nothing like putting it to the test. King set off in the storm for a two-story building farther along the street, which housed the company offices. This was Saturday night, and the company observed the Sabbath to the extent that no regular work was done on Sunday. So he hoped to see Apperson today, if possible.

A couple of weary clerks were still at their desks, but the general foreman had departed some time before, and they did not expect him back. There was a possibility they might find him at his room at the hotel.

King gathered that it was no more than a possibility, but he made the try. Mitchell, the clerk, recognizing him, looked hastily about to make sure that King was alone.

"I'm mighty sorry about makin' a fool of myself, about you and the lady," he apologized anew. "I just sort of took it for granted—"

"That's all right," King assured him. She found a

room with Mrs. Travis across the street."

"Now why didn't I think of Mis' Travis? Best place in the whole durned town. I'd sure like to board over there myself. No other place to eat that's half as good, though Charley's, up at the halfway stop—"

"I'm looking for Bart Apperson," King interrupted. "Is—"

"Lookin' for a job haulin' ore, eh? I saw your wagons. Well, you ought to get it—if that's what you want."

"Why shouldn't I want it?"

Mitchell shrugged. "I guess a man has to eat these days," he acknowledged, "though some figure they'd sooner starve. Course, Bart Apperson rooms here, but I ain't beholden to him. All I was meanin' is that a bunch of teamsters quit and pulled out a couple of days back, which leaves him shorthanded, so he'll need more, all right.

That information was by way of being both encouraging and disquieting. King let it pass.

"Is he in his room?"

At this time of day? Be the first time it ever happened, if he was. There's always parties, Saturday night, and Bart's the shinin' light of this camp, so he don't aim to hide his light under no bushel of spuds. Likely you'll find him at one of them."

Parties, King gathered, was a rather loose term. There was money in Silverhill, more than in most communities across the land, and on Saturday nights those who had it felt impelled to celebrate their good fortune.

Further inquiry indicated that there was no telling where Apperson might be. He had a way of getting around. So King began the rounds himself.

Wilma was feeling neglected. With her, it was not a new sensation. She could be talking and laughing, the center of a group of people, and still feel that way. It depended on who was in the group, and whether their attention was centered on her or she was only one of the group. Wilma disliked being one flower in a cluster. She preferred to be the flower about whom men clustered.

She was one of a group now, but there was no one in particular gathering who interested her. There were miners, muckers, teamsters—run of the mill men, and even more run of the mill women. Smiling and chatting, Wilma looked about speculatively. If only someone new would put in an appearance—

Her eyes, brown as autumn nuts, widened suddenly, and she caught her breath. It couldn't be—but it was— the very man she'd been thinking about, remembering with a touch of nostalgia. There could be no mistake, even after half a dozen years. He was too big, too outstanding, even in a crowd, to be mistaken or to be forgotten. Her breath caught again. Maybe she'd been a fool not to hang on to him when she'd had the chance—

He was looking around, obviously seeking someone. Wilma waited, holding her breath, then let it out in a slow sigh. Her back was partly turned, and another of the men had moved between them at the wrong moment. King Coleman hadn't seen her. Her hands clasped, and she twisted the ring on her finger. The gesture was involuntary, but with sudden determination she wrenched it off and as swiftly concealed it. Then, smiling, she started toward him, disregarding those with whom she had been talking.

Not finding whoever he was seeking, King was already turning back to the door. He started as a hand was laid on his arm and a voice spoke breathlessly:

"King! It *is* you! I knew I couldn't be mistaken!"

Coleman turned, surprised. Then his grin flashed with pleasure as he recognized the woman smiling up at him.

"Wilma!" he marveled. "Now where in the world did you come from?"

"I might ask the same of you," she returned gaily. "Here I'm feeling lonesome, and *you* walk in! It's like the answer to a maiden's prayer. Let's go where we can talk."

She had always been expert at finding a nook or corner when that was possible. King followed her lead and sank into a chair beside her.

"I sure didn't expect to find you in this camp, Wilma," he said. "It's about the last place I'd look for you."

"Why?" she challenged. "There's more going on here than most places, these days. And *you're* here!"

King shrugged. "I fit. There's the difference."

"Maybe I do, too." She made it plain that she was genuinely glad to see him. "What have you been doing, King? It's been quite a while."

"So it has." He did not add, *Too long.* "Not much. Getting the ranch I always wanted, a little spread out from Stockton. As to why I'm here, there's ore to be hauled, and I've a few teams and wagons."

He had no intention of making it sound glamorous or impressive. It was the simple truth, no more. But beauty is in the eye of the beholder, and interpretation in the ear and the wish. A man who had a ranch and a string of wagons was getting on in the world. She had expected that of King Coleman, of course. He'd been that sort.

Talking excitedly, her mind reviewed the possibilities, and King listened, pleased. It was nice to meet an old friend—and Wilma, in her day, had been rather special. He'd tried about every place he could think of or which others could suggest, but he had no luck in finding Apperson. So seeing the foreman would have to wait; besides, it wasn't too important.

"Let's get out of here," Wilma suggested excitedly,

and got to her feet, smiling into his eyes. "Let's go some place where we can *really* talk! We've got much to say to each other."

King doubted that. He'd already said about all he had to say to her. The glow was gone from the rose.

But he was a notoriously good-natured man. He would go out of his way to avoid giving disappointment, and if Wilma was lonesome, as she seemed to be, he had no objection to being friendly. He followed her out into the night, noting that the rain was slackening. The street outside was inky.

"It's so awfully dark!" she whispered. "But here we are. Wait while I get a light."

She opened a door abruptly, right off the street, and King heard her fumbling in the gloom. Then a match cast a red glow, was transferred to the wick of a lamp, and sprang to full bloom as the chimney was set above the flame.

"I live here," she answered his look of inquiry. "A girl has to have a place," she added defensively. "Only men are at the hotel."

"Sure, I know," he agreed. "Looks like a nice place you have."

"It's not bad," she conceded. "Wait while I stir up the fire and get some coffee. It's so cold and wet."

She had hurried out early, but to her pleased surprise there was still some fire in the big range, and she soon had it stirred to a glow. She bustled about excitedly, shoving the coffeepot over the flame, finding half a pie and slicing a generous wedge to set before him. The coffee had been boiled and reboiled, but she remembered that he liked his strong. Cowboys always did.

King ate the pie, listening to her talk. It was a pleasant drone, like the chatter of magpies. Once he'd liked it. Now it wouldn't take long to get too much of it. He wiped his mouth and stood up.

"That was sure good pie," he said. "And thanks for the coffee." He was a big man, smiling quizzically. "You've learned how to cook, Wilma. That pie's an improvement over the one you made me another time. Remember?"

She colored, then laughed. Her mother had told her that the way to a man's heart was through his stomach, so she'd labored valiantly over a pie—and he had labored as valiantly trying to down a slice of it. He'd been a good sport, and in love.

"You poor boy!" she said. "I almost poisoned you, didn't I?" She reached up suddenly, put her hands on his cheeks and kissed him quickly. "I'm better now, as you say. Must you go so soon?"

"Got to be hitting the hay," he said. "It's been a long day. I expect I'll be seeing you, Wilma."

"You certainly will," she agreed. "It's been wonderful, King—and now that we're both in the same town—"

She stood in the open doorway to call good night. Before it closed, a man came past, cat-footed in the night. In the light from the doorway, King caught a glimpse of his face, tight with a sardonic smile. It was the boarder who had been so officious at Mrs. Travis': DeQuille.

3

Having shaken the hay from his clothes and found a chance to shave, King surveyed himself regretfully in the cracked mirror in the stable office. The shave helped, but he was suddenly conscious he needed to spruce up. The trouble was that there wasn't much he could do. But the prospect of seeing Vicki at the breakfast table almost made up for that.

Clouds still hung across the valley, shutting out the view of Helltop, and there was a chill bite to the air. For the most part the town was asleep at that hour on a Sunday. He reached Maggie Travis' and let himself in, to be greeted by Vicki herself. For a moment he stared, unbelieving.

She had on a fresh dress and, after her bedraggled appearance of the day before, was wholly lovely. Finding his voice, he said as much.

"I knew you were beautiful yesterday," he murmured, and his tone was reverent. "But I didn't guess the half of it!"

Vicki colored, but it was plain that she had no intention of taking him too seriously.

"Moon was warning me that you have the gift of gab," she retorted; "a smooth tongue laced with soap. I suppose it all adds up to your being hungry."

"Well, now, I could do with breakfast, for a fact—particularly if I may have such charming company while I eat," King conceded. "But as for Moon, let me set you straight. While I revere the old gentleman and love him dearly, still his word on such subjects is as undependable as the chatter of a jaybird upon a limb."

"Did you find Mr. Apperson last evening?"

"Bart Apperson is like a flea, it would appear. You go to place your finger down, and the place wherein he was is vacant. But I hope to discover him this morning."

"I hope you do," Vicki agreed. "I hope you and Moon get the job."

"The job I will have," King promised. "Why this show of confidence? Since yesterday my luck is running high, wide and handsome."

It was an excellent breakfast. He had no notion what he ate, but no other boarders showed up until he had finished. By that time, King knew the truth beyond doubt—he was in love, really in love, for the first time in his life. Compared to this, the infatuation for Wilma was like a pale candle beside the noonday sun. He wanted to tell Vicki so, but his better judgment prevailed, as well as the presence of several newcomers. He took his leave.

Bob Mitchell, the clerk at the Palace, confirmed that Apperson had returned to his room and should be stirring at any time. King waited, and after almost an hour, Apperson came down the stairs.

He was preparing to shave, and his eyes looked red. He shrank as Mitchell hailed him boomingly, pointing out King and explaining that he had been waiting to see him. Apperson's glance was hardly enthusiastic.

"Ah!" he observed. "You're Coleman, eh? But this is Sunday."

"I tried to find you last night," King explained. "No luck. I'm here with my teams and wagons, and we want to make sure of the job. We're ready to go to work in the morning."

"Ah." Apperson pondered. "Yes," he added, "you wrote me. But you may recall that I said that the jobs which were available would go to whoever came first."

King's mood, soaring like a balloon, suffered deflation. It was quite plain that Apperson didn't particularly like him, and he shared the feeling. But Apperson was boss. That was to be remembered.

"Do you mean that somebody was ahead of us?" he asked.

"Well—yes and no." Apperson's eyes were blue, but

it was the blue of a winter sky just before a blizzard. "I play no favorites. I had word yesterday about another man who is coming with a dozen wagons. He is resting at Tenbrook today, but should be in tomorrow. It creates a problem, you see—for there won't be enough work for both of you."

"We're here first," King pointed out.

"Ah—yes. And no. He sent word first—which, in a sense, makes it a dead heat, you might say."

Definitely, King did not like this big mogul.

"Times are hard," Apperson went on. "If there is a surplus of labor, wagons, teams—I might not be able to pay quite the rate I discussed in the letter. Reardon, sending me word that he was at Tenbrook, suggested that he wanted the job badly enough to work for a lower rate." He eyed King speculatively, and when Coleman did not rise to the bait, concluded, "Let's see tomorrow, eh—after he gets here?"

Tenbrook lay some eighteen miles to the south. It was the only town on the road to the smelter. Securing a horse at the livery stable, King rode quietly out from the camp. It might be a wise precaution to have a conference with this other man, Reardon. Otherwise Apperson would have them over a barrel.

It was noon when he reached Tenbrook, a town small enough to be surveyed in one searching glance. Sunshine had pushed the clouds aside, and Tenbrook

showed as a wide flat space. There were no waiting wagons in the town, nor had he encountered any along the
road.

There was a restaurant, patronized by haulers on
weekdays, sleepily quiet today. The food lacked the
touch of Maggie Travis, but inquiries brought food for
thought. There had been no such wagons as Apperson
had described, nor had such a man as Reardon been
heard of. The cook was blunt.

"There ain't been any such man along here, nor there
won't be. Why should there? A man'd be a fool to
come huntin' work at the mines. I know—I mucked
there a spell. And the only work there's what Apperson
chooses to give. Me, I'd sooner starve than go back to
slavin' for him."

There was no competition, but King was uncertain
whether or not the information was encouraging. He
turned back, riding thoughtfully. He had left the town
a mile behind when a pair of horsemen emerged from a
cluster of trees. Both were masked, and each clutched
a six-gun. But his first supposition that it was a holdup
was dissipated by the opening remark:

"So you had to come snoopin', eh? Wanted to see
for yourself about those wagons, eh? Well, you've had
your look—and how much good do you think it's going
to do you?"

It was plain that Apperson had set the pair to watch

him when he'd ridden out of the camp. King hadn't
supposed that the foreman would be sufficiently concerned, one way or another, to take such a drastic step.
Now it was plain that he had underestimated Apperson.
The foreman's control was maintained not only by economic pressure but also by a spy system.

"Is there any law against a man going for a ride?"
King asked mildly. "I hadn't heard about it."

"You're hearin' now, mister. You'd have been smarter
to take the word you had and let it go at that. Climb
down off your horse."

King sighed. With two guns on him, it was necessary
to comply. It had been a long while since he'd carried
a gun, and it hadn't occurred to him that one might be
necessary.

"I wish you'd tell me what's wrong," he said plain-
tively. "Here I thought it would be a good idea to get
familiar with the road I'm to be hauling over, but you
seem to think that's a sin."

His pretense of innocence was partly successful; at
least it caused them to relax their vigilance. One thrust
his gun contemptuously back into the holster, and the
second man allowed his own to waver. Then he started
to swing it in a quick, vicious arc which would bring
the flat of the barrel alongside King's skull.

King had other ideas. His own movements were even
faster than the lash of the gun. He ducked and side-

stepped, lunging forward, and the swish of the barrel
fanned empty space. The force of the blow left the gun-
man momentarily off balance. A moment was enough.
King's shoulder caught the fellow broadside in a driving lunge, spilling him to the road.

That was half of the maneuver. The other part con-
sisted of a sidewise kick. King's boot heel drove deep
into the second man's middle, causing him to make a
sound like a blow-up sack being popped. He, too, sat
down.

One revolver was on the road. King picked it up,
then helped himself to the other, while its owner
blinked up at him with the look of a hurt puppy, clasping his hands about his middle and groaning. King
slipped the guns into his coat pockets, grinning down
at them.

"All through so soon?" he chided. "I thought you
wanted to play. This way, you spoil the fun. If you'd
like to have a game of tiddlywinks some time, just let
me know. Always glad to oblige."

He stooped suddenly and plucked the bandana from
the face of the man who still gasped from his kick.
Watery blue eyes blinked at him, but the face was un-
familiar.

The man who had tried to pistol-whip him jumped
up suddenly and dashed for his horse. He scrambled
into the saddle and kicked the cayuse wildly into mo-

tion. King watched with wry amusement. Unless he chose to shoot, or to go to the trouble of pursuing, he couldn't stop him, and he doubted that a look at the other man's face would be worth the effort.

"He must have a mighty homely mug." King sighed. "I'll leave your guns at Pete's Place," he informed the other man, "in case you want to call for them." He crossed to his own horse and mounted.

"But I wouldn't carry a gun again if I was you. A gun's a risky toy if you don't know how to use it."

He headed back to town, stopping at the bar known as Pete's Place, then crossed to the hotel. On the way he encountered Moon, a worried set to his mustache.

"Where've you been, King?" he asked. "I've been lookin' for you. I'm afraid I've bad news."

"Seems like most news fits that description," King observed. "What's the bad part of this?"

"I ran into Apperson on the street a while ago, so I introduced myself. He says if we want to go to work in the morning, we'll have to do it for eight bucks a day per wagon; not ten. Too many others willing to work for that price." Moon shook his head. "We can't up and pull out of here right now—for a lot of reasons. But we can't make a cent at that rate."

"I'll have a talk with him," King said. "I've sort of a hunch that I can talk him into paying the rate he promised."

"You ever tried arguin' with a rattlesnake?" Moon asked dryly.

"It's not a rattlin' good proposition," King agreed. "But I feel mighty persuasive today."

"Want I should come along?"

"If you're willing to leave it to me, I'll endeavor to point out the error of his ways—gently, of course," King added, seeing the worry in Moon's eyes. "See you later."

Mitchell confirmed the fact that Apperson was in his room.

"Want I should beller up for him?" he asked helpfully. "Tell him you're comin'?"

"The pleasure will probably be double if it's unexpected," King told him. "I'll announce myself." He climbed the stairs, rapped, and at an invitation to enter, did so. Apperson, busily adjusting a tie before a mirror, swung about, and for a moment his jaw sagged.

"I'm in excellent health, since I know you're anxious about it," King assured him. "And your boys are hardly mussed up, either, which is rather a pity. If they'd only shown a little more enthusiasm, I'd have been glad to get some exercise."

"I don't know what you're talking about," Apperson blustered. But he could not keep the uneasiness from his tone.

"In that case, no matter." King waved airily. "I'll

start hauling in the morning—at the rate we agreed on to start with. You'll need our wagons, since Reardon has done a vanishing act."

The foreman shrugged.

"If you want to go to work, all right," he agreed. "Do the job right and there'll be no complaint. That's all I ask. You'll all get loads up at the mines. Now, if you'll excuse me, I'm busy."

King was thoughtful as he made his way back to the street.

4.

Vicki was waiting on table when King arrived for breakfast the next morning. Her face was flushed from bending over the stove, and she flashed him a smile as he hung up his hat and coat. The room was already filled.

"So many people to feed make a lot of extra work," Vicki explained. "Lena is willing, but still strange to our way of doing, so I'm helping out temporarily. Maggie is treating me as though I were her daughter, and I want to show my appreciation."

"It sure looks as though you've found the way to do it," King agreed. "You know, those roses in your cheeks make me think I've come to the banana belt."

"Moon says you kissed the Blarney stone, and apparently he's right," Vicki returned, but her smile disclosed a dimple as she sped back to the kitchen. King, sliding into a chair, encountered a scowl on the face of DeQuille, seated across the table. He, in common with most of the other boarders, appeared smitten by Vicki's charms.

Moon came in from the kitchen. He looked abashed as he met King's gaze, but the look of contentment on his face was too deep to be easily masked. Dan O'Leary caught it and asked an innocent question of Flood, beside him.

"Do you figure, Mike, that bein' a boardin' house landlord's a good job?"

Flood considered the question. "Might be," he conceded. "A man would always know where his next meal was comin' from. But we got a land*lady*," he added.

"Yeah—but there's such a thing as havin' both," O'Leary pointed out. "What does the Good Book say? When you see signs an' wonders, you know winter's on the way."

"I ain't what you'd classify as an expert on what it says, but I doubt if that's the way it goes," Mike returned dubiously.

Moon choked. "Gosh, that coffee's hot," he observed, and slid back his chair. "Come on, you yahoos. Time to get rollin'. We've work to do."

O'Leary paused to speak to Lena in Danish as she came from the kitchen, flashing a grin at Moon. Once the teams were hitched, King explained the program.

"We go on the hill after ore," he said. "Nothing to do but ride up and down. The horses do all the work."

He led the way, falling in behind another string of wagons beginning the ascent. The sky was clear, the air frosty. Along the street the mud was beginning to dry. It was just daylight, but there below the hill the sun would not show for another hour. A little later in the season they'd be setting out in the dark.

King's suspicion that it might be rough was borne out as the road climbed. Helltop towered nearly four thousand feet above the town. In a straight line, up and down, it wasn't a great distance, but by road it was a five-mile journey. At that, the trail was often sharp and steep.

The horses had to pull, even with an empty wagon. Coming down, they'd have to set back in the traces and hold hard, despite the brakes. If anything went wrong, disaster could pounce like a leaping puma. A man would be lucky to be able to jump before his wagon went over the side. Several had done that since the mines had commenced operations. The hill had not acquired its name for nothing.

There were occasional places where the road widened so that two wagons could pass, but for much of the distance there was no room to spare even for one vehicle. The wagons went up twice a day, morning and afternoon. After all were up and loaded, they came down. No vehicles were allowed to travel in the opposite direction once the trip had begun.

After making the descent with a load of ore, the wagons went on to the smelter, and others took their place. The trip out was an easy one compared to the descent.

A third of the way up the hill, King was surprised to encounter a line of men, trudging upward. It was the day crew, going up to dig ore. There was no stage or other conveyance for their accommodation. Apparently the men walked to work, then trudged down again when their ten-hour shift was finished. It was necessary to go so far because there had been no chance to build a town closer than the foot of the hill. Helltop was too rugged for that.

The line of wagons ahead passed the men without stopping, the horses walking faster than the men chose to climb. For the most part, the miners did not even look up; merely moved to the side to permit the wagons to pass. King hailed them.

"Wouldn't you fellows like a ride?" He pulled to a stop. "Pile on, 'less you're too proud to travel in such a rig. These horses ain't half earnin' their keep with an empty wagon."

Faces were raised now, surprise plain on them. Then the men came scrambling aboard. One settled onto the seat beside King, and others seated themselves on the floor of the wagon box, unmindful of the jolting.

"Gee, mister, this is mighty white of you," the man

beside him said. "It gets to be a long way up this hill, and there's a mighty long day afterward."

Others were boarding the wagons which came behind, but those ahead continued to pass up the climbers. King shook his head in perplexity.

"No reason why you shouldn't ride, is there? I'd sure appreciate a lift, if I had to get up there."

"Anybody would," the miner agreed. "But it just ain't the custom."

"Why not? Don't you fellows wipe your boots clean or something?"

He was rewarded with a faint grin. "You're new here, ain't you?"

"Guess I must be."

"And you're started haulin' off Helltop, first off! Man, how'd you get this job?"

"Meanin'?"

"I don't know. Only the rule is—no riders. But when it comes to takin' a wagon out, every new man is supposed to be broken in on a few trips out to the smelter, after the ore's down at the camp. If they do that all right, then they can tackle the hill."

"I've seen hills before," King said. "But why the rule against men riding the wagons up?"

"Mebby it ain't exactly the law, but it's the custom. Now you know, do you want we should get down?"

"If you don't like my company, all right," King replied. "But when I ask a man to ride, I don't kick him off."

"You must be this King Cole people are talkin' about. I'm Baker—Hard Rock, my friends call me."

King extended his hand. "A man can use friends," he said simply.

Baker's craggy face relaxed in a smile. "You've made yourself some," he said, and fumbled with a sack of the makin's. "Want I should roll you one?" he asked, as he spilled tobacco into a paper and licked it smooth with an expert tongue.

King shook his head. "Thanks, but I guess I'll be smokin' enough up here without."

"You sure will, if you keep on like you've started."

"I was thinkin' of the weather." It had been comparatively warm, even at dawn, in the town. As they climbed, there was a noticeable change. By the time they reached the crest, he'd be able to see his breath. Baker nodded.

"Sure makes a lot of difference," he conceded. "Down at the camp, on a summer night, you swelter. Up here it's plenty cool. And in the winter, which'll hit up here any day—you'd think it was the north pole. That's why I like workin' underground. Always warm there."

There was a widening in the road, a flat bench about an acre in extent. One building stood at the side, the sign proclaiming it to be Charley's Place. The halfway

house was popular for refreshments both on the way up
and the way down. Some of the night crew had come
that far and were pausing for breakfast or a cup of coffee before completing the descent.

As they continued to climb, the road grew steeper,
the curves sharper. Even in good weather it was a tricky
thoroughfare, and could easily be treacherous.

"This must be something when it gets icy," King
suggested. Baker grinned through a fog of smoke.

"Yeah—special with a blizzard spittin' like seventeen
cats and the wind blowin' your whiskers loose!"

They reached the top and pulled to a stop, waiting
their turn to load. Immediately below was the gash
of a canyon, splitting into more fissures, the depths lost
in the gloom and shadows. Posts and a heavy log railing had been erected beside the road, but even with
that protection, it was a long way down.

The ore chute was ahead, its snout extending over
the road. The chute had been rigged of heavy planks,
bringing the ore down from three mines another hundred yards or so on up the hill. The wagons would
drive under, and an operator would tug a rope to raise
a gate, allowing the heavy ore to thunder down into the
wagon, then slap the gate closed again.

Off at the side, part way up the slope, was the change
house, where the miners changed from street clothes
to the garments they used while digging and back

again. It was all crude—more so than any similar operation King had ever seen, and he was not entirely a stranger to that sort of thing.

The miners thanked him and piled out, trudging off to the change house. Dan O'Leary, next in line, came up to talk.

"What do you make of it, King?" he asked. "The boys tell me it's against the rules to give rides. What sort of a place is this? And they say newcomers are never assigned to work on the hill till they've proved themselves on a few trips to the smelter. There's something funny here."

"I guess I'm to blame," King said soberly. "I had a run-in with the boss. He wanted us to work at a cut rate, and I sort of got him over a barrel. So we can work —but he's showing his displeasure."

"So that's it? It strikes me, King, that we're workin' for a second cousin to a skunk."

"I got you boys into this." King sighed. "If you'd rather go back to the ranch, I won't say a word against it."

O'Leary swore. "You know that wasn't what I was drivin' at, King," he protested. "It's just that I like to smell clean air. But if you ride these roads, we'll be right with you. And if you want to take on Bart Apperson and his whole blasted crew—why, they'll find they didn't know the meanin' of Helltop up to now!"

A louder clatter caught King's attention, and it did not come from the ore chute. More ore was smashing down a separate wooden chute, but not toward the wagons. He saw it pour from the lip of the chute, spill into a canyon and plunge from sight far below. Now it was his turn to load. He jerked a thumb toward the loader and asked a question.

"What's that?"

The loader spat, studying him through eyes which reminded King of a weasel's.

"Waste," he said briefly. "Pull up a little more. Hold it. Steady your horses! Lots of waste," he added. The ore came crashing down, shaking the wagon, quickly filling the triple tier of boxes. Expertly he gauged it, shut off the flow and gestured King onward.

King was thoughtful as he drove. Twice more, before a bend of the hill blanketed the sound, he heard the roar of waste being dumped. Naturally there would be a lot of waste. But how much, he wondered, was waste, and how much good ore was being discarded so prodigally? He doubted if the facilities at the mine were adequate to make a careful separation. The difference between profit and loss could lie right there.

Perhaps it was none of his business. He was hired to haul, and that was all. Still, a man couldn't help thinking—and wondering.

The hill was tricky, but not too bad for a man who

knew his business. King's horses were big animals, well broken, and they knew when to set back in the traces and plant their huge hoofs solidly. Given half a chance, they could hold a load even without the brakes. But when there was ice and storm, it would be a chancy business. The first job at day's end would be to get them all sharp-shod.

The other wagons were halting at Charley's, so he took his turn, pulling to the side, tying one lead horse at a post, then ducking inside. The room was big, low-ceilinged, misty with a perpetual haze of smoke. There was a counter and tables. Charley appeared from the kitchen, a bland-faced Oriental with a long pigtail. His eyes fixed inscrutably on King for a moment, but no emotion showed there.

His coffee was good, and the food looked appetizing. King returned to his wagon and went on down. The road leveled as they came into Silverhill. O'Leary, be-hind him, mopped his face and shouted:

"That was what I needed to settle my breakfast! But I'll not be mad at any easy road for a while."

King did not reply. Apperson was approaching, walking with the brisk air of a busy man. He nodded curtly.

"Have a good trip down?" he asked, and climbed onto a brake block to peer over at the ore. Not waiting for a reply, he gestured toward the big stable-yard, where extra wagons stood in rows.

"You boys take some of those wagons for the afternoon trip. Others will take these loads on to the smelter. You'll get your own wagons back in regular rotation."

"What do you mean?" King demanded. "They tell me that the rule is: when a man brings a wagon down, he makes the trip all the way."

Apperson shrugged. "That's usually the case," he conceded. "But we're doing it this way now."

"These are my wagons—and I don't like turnin' them over to other drivers," King said slowly, fighting his temper.

"Nothing will happen to your wagons," Apperson retorted. "If anything does, they will be replaced. You're drivin' the hill for the present. And while we're on that subject—we don't encourage giving rides to the men. Too dangerous."

King eyed him levelly. "If we're drivin' the hill, we're drivin' it. And if they're willing to risk ridin' up with me, I figure that's my business!"

Apperson shrugged. "It'll get you disliked by the others you have to work with," he warned, and turned away. King broke the news to the other drivers as they came up.

"The boss doesn't like me," he explained. "So he's showin' it that way—and the rest of you have to bear the brunt of it."

Flood spat.

"Who's complainin'?" he asked. "All we have to do is ride up and down. The horses do all the work—and half the time, they're walkin' downhill."

The afternoon trip was routine; the sun was shining warmly. One wagon was much like another, and these had to be strongly built to stand the shock of the ore from the loading chute, and the strain of the long haul to the smelter. Now, while the road was good and the weather co-operative, hauling down the hill wasn't bad.

Vicki was again waiting on table at supper. She flashed King a smile, but was too busy for more. Feeding two dozen hungry men and keeping the tables supplied was a full-time job. Lena remained in the kitchen, helping Maggie.

The men were in a relaxed mood, tired at day's end but with the knowledge that rest lay ahead.

DeQuille was openly watching Vicki as she came and went, trying to get her attention, to draw a smile. When these efforts failed, he reached out suddenly and closed his fingers about her wrist.

"What's your hurry, honey?" he asked. "We're well provided with food, but we're starvin' for a smile. Here, sit down and talk a while—my lap 'll do fine."

Vicki's face lost color, then flooded an angry red. She struggled ineffectually to free herself. Faces turned as King scraped back his chair. In that moment he loomed bigger than usual.

"Take your dirty paws off her!" he ordered. "And leave her alone!"

DeQuille obeyed the first part of the injunction, but his look matched his tone in insolence as he swung to survey his challenger.

"Listen to who's talkin'!" he jeered. "What business is it of yours, mister? You have another girl, and her another man's wife!"

5.

King felt his neck reddening; then his face went white. With sickening clarity he understood. DeQuille had seen him leaving that other house in the night, had recognized him and known whose place it was. Now he was trading on that to put King in his place.

But the rest of it—his assertion that the other woman was another man's wife! King hadn't thought to ask Wilma, and she hadn't volunteered any information, but it was logical. Otherwise why would she be living there, in a town where men outnumbered the women ten to one, and in a house of her own?

"What the devil are you talking about?" King jerked out, and knew that it was the wrong question. He'd been cornered without realizing it.

"What am I talking about?" DeQuille repeated. "Why, nothing much, Romeo. Only about you squirin' the mine foreman's wife when he's away on shift. Mrs. Yount—Wilma, as you call her—mighty familiar." He shrugged. "I reckon that's your business—yours and Yount's, mebby. But if it is, then this ain't!"

Vicki had retreated to the kitchen, her cheeks vivid, casting a look at him in which shock and incredulity mingled. King remained standing, his jaw muscles ridged, holding himself in check with an effort.

DeQuille pushed back his own chair, grinning sardonically. He crossed the room and lifted down hat and coat from the rack, shrugging into the coat.

"Cat got your tongue, Romeo?" he taunted. "Well, it's none of my business." He sauntered to the door and out. The others were eating in silence, or rising, embarrassed, to slip out. King watched a minute, while the tiredness of the day settled like sand in his muscles. Then, leaving the remainder of his supper untasted, he went through the door to the kitchen.

The clatter of pans and dishes had stilled there, then resumed almost on a note of ferocity. King felt his face burn again as he saw the three women, each studiously busy about some task. Ignoring the others, he addressed himself to Vicki.

"Mebby he's tellin' the truth—as he sees it," he conceded. "All I know is that I was lookin' for Apperson night before last, and at a party I ran into this girl— Wilma. I used to know her, years ago. We talked, naturally, and she asked me to take her home, then to have a cup of coffee. She didn't tell me she was married, and I didn't think to ask."

He wanted to add that she had been wearing no ring, but that, like the other part, would sound more damning than it was.

"That's all there was to it," he added. "Honest."

Vicki looked at him, and in her eyes was belief. But she was a woman, and had been almost as humiliated as himself. She could not resist a small revenge.

"If she's an old friend, of course you'd be glad to see her," she agreed. "But what you do, or whom you choose to see, is certainly your own affair and none of mine."

She walked through another door and disappeared, and he had no way of guessing that it took an effort to hold her shoulders straight, to keep them from heaving uncontrollably as soon as the door was shut. King swung about and snatched his coat. He knew a rebuff when he heard one. The worst of it was, he couldn't blame her.

Night had closed again, but the sky was uncluttered by clouds and the moon had waxed, so that the street was no longer a fog of blackness. The door to Pete's Place stood open, and light made a ragged pool on the sidewalk. Farther on, a general store was having its busiest hour of the day. A lantern was suspended from a beam above the sidewalk, making another break in the gloom.

It was his luck, as he came under the lantern, to encounter Wilma emerging from the store.

King cursed under his breath. In his present mood, Wilma was the last person he cared to see. But he couldn't duck and run. He'd always been stubborn about retreating, even when that seemed the feasible course. She had seen him, and was exclaiming eagerly.

"King! Now this is luck! I've been wondering why you didn't look me up again.

She fell into step alongside him, tendering the packages she was carrying, and King took them automatically.

"What's this I hear about you being married, Wilma?" he asked without preamble.

She halted; then her laugh came.

"Is that what's worrying you?" she asked. "Yes, I'm married—they say everybody makes a fool of himself at least once!" Her tone was bitter. "I've had my turn. But that doesn't affect the fact that we're old friends, does it, King? Or that I'm awfully glad to see you, and desperately lonely?"

He was moved by what she said, moved and sorry. But his anger remained.

"A married woman usually wears a ring," he said.

"A ring? Oh, you mean a wedding ring? I lost mine only Saturday, King. Yount was furious—he seemed to think I did it deliberately. I took it off when I kneaded bread dough, and somehow it disappeared. I'm sorry if you got the wrong impression—"

They were still walking. King was acutely uncomfortable. It was one thing to be sorry for her, because she'd made a mistake and was unhappy. But he had no intention of interfering between man and wife, and in any case there was nothing he could do. Such affairs were not for outsiders to meddle in.

He realized that they were stopping before her door, that she was opening it and fumbling again for a light. With his arms full, he had no choice but to step in and deposit the bundles on the kitchen table. Yount, he reflected sardonically, was probably off on Helltop again.

He was turning back to the door when she stopped him.

"Don't go, King—not yet. I've got to talk to you. I'll fix coffee—"

"I've just had my supper," he said hastily. "And if your husband is jealous, like you suggest, I shouldn't be hangin' around here."

Wilma tossed her head. "Are you afraid of him?" she asked, and the words were half a taunt. "He's big— but you could eat him. But he's away for the night again. And I—don't go, King. I've got to talk things over with someone. I can't go on this way."

Against his will, he took a chair and waited. Since he was there, better to have it settled and done with.

"Just how bad is it?" he asked. "You seem to have a nice house here—a right good home for this part of the country—"

"It's a good house, but a house doesn't make a home!" she broke in. "Can't you see, King—I made a mistake, as I told you. I've tried to make the best of it, but it has become so bad that I can't keep on."

"I'm sorry if that's the way it is," King said. "But as long as you're married to him, Wilma, I can't come here. It would just make bad matters worse."

It was an unfortunate choice of words. She cried eagerly:

"But I won't stay married to him, King! I'll leave him—tonight, if you say so. I'll get a divorce. People will talk, I suppose, but I'm past caring. They're always doing it anyhow. And you're strange here, so it shouldn't make any difference to you, especially since we've found each other again—"

Something in his face stopped her. He stood at the door, and he seemed to tower. Her tongue had slipped that time. *They're always doing it anyhow!* That phrase was far more revealing than she'd intended. If Yount was jealous, if there was trouble between them, King could understand why.

Once he'd liked her, but two nights ago he'd discovered that the embers were cold and dead. Now he realized that what he felt was a growing dislike. But he tried to keep that from his voice.

"I'm sorry, Wilma," he said; "sorry if you're unhappy and having trouble. But let's not have any misunderstanding. You picked another man—and I like another woman. I'd still like to be friends, to help you if I can—but not that way. You'll see for yourself, when you stop to think it over, that it wouldn't work, not for either of us."

He opened the door and let himself out into the night. The coffeepot was boiling over, spilling unnoticed on the stove. The light in her eyes was not calculated to remind him of roses and moonlight. He'd never seen eyes so.

"A woman scorned," he muttered. "Whoosh! The more you try to get in the clear, man, the deeper you sink!" He drew a long breath. "One time you were sure lucky—you might have been fooled into marryin' her!"

The weather continued good, and the work was becoming routine.

In mid-week, word came that there'd be no hauling to do that day. All easy or available ore had been mucked out; it was necessary now to drill, then to set off a series of blasts and loosen up a fresh supply. That happened every now and then. Usually the blasting was done over Sunday, to avoid delays, but sometimes the supply didn't last the week out.

That meant a day with no pay for miners and haulers

alike, but there was no choice. It struck King that there was an unnecessary lack of efficiency in the operation of the mines. Either Apperson and his top men, such as Yount, didn't really know their jobs, or else there was a deliberate intent to see that the mines showed no real profit.

King hadn't made up his mind which; it could be a combination of both factors. But the day off gave him a chance to look about, to satisfy his curiosity on certain points.

He hesitated, more abashed than he'd felt in a long while. It was going to be another nice day, and he'd enjoy it twice as much if Vicki would accompany him on the hike he intended to take. But there had been a certain reserve between them since DeQuille had shot off his mouth—

Well, the sooner that misunderstanding was cleared up, the better. He rose from the breakfast table and turned to the kitchen.

"Vicki around?" he asked. It occurred to him that he hadn't seen her that morning.

Maggie Travis wiped her hands on her apron. Since King was Moon's partner, she was friendly.

"No, she ain't," she said. "DeQuille found out there wasn't to be any work today and said something to her —I don't know what. I saw them go off together a little while ago."

"In that case," King said, "I won't see her just yet."

He hoped it sounded airy; it wasn't up to him to carry his heart on his sleeve. He was turning back when Maggie stopped him.

"Why don't you say it?" she demanded. "I would myself, if I wasn't a lady. I'm disappointed, King. I thought she had better sense."

King cocked a crooked eyebrow at her. As a long-time boarder, am I to gather that DeQuille still falls short of being a favorite?"

"The man has to eat, and so do I!" Maggie said vehemently. "As long as he pays his bills and behaves himself within reason, I can't complain. But that doesn't make me like him. He's a lickspittle!"

King was grinning to himself as he went outside. The lines of worry that had been etching themselves across Moon's face had largely smoothed away in the last few days. That was Maggie's doing, and she was a woman with the judgment and the other qualities to make a lasting and favorable impression.

King set out on foot, following the road to where it commenced to climb, then leaving it behind. Almost at once he was in rugged country where a man had to be a mountaineer if he hoped to progress. A tenderfoot, or a man raised only on the prairie or in the woods, would be baffled by such terrain. King had spent a lot of time studying the larger features of the valley as he rode the wagon, and he had them well in mind. Even so, progress was difficult.

It was mid-morning when he arrived at his goal, back in the depths of a canyon. Despite what he'd been prepared to find, he whistled in surprise. Here was the waste which was dumped as the mining progressed. After leaving the chute far above, it rolled and bounced and slid and tumbled for well over a mile; shunted aside by the walls of intersecting canyons, it finally ended up here. The growing pile was of respectable size —he estimated it to be thousands of tons.

King climbed about, picking up an occasional chunk. It was safe to prowl there today, since no more waste was being dumped. Some was nothing more than rock, obviously waste. But a great deal of it looked to his untutored eyes as good as most of the ore he'd been hauling. It was very heavy, dark—and that appeared to be the main difference between it and what they were using.

On a hunch, he loaded his pockets with samples from various parts of the heap, then spent another hour looking about.

If his hunch should be right—King grinned. Now he was really getting ideas. But it would do no harm to find out.

He turned and commenced climbing, finally reaching Charley's Place at the halfway point. Today the restaurant was almost empty. He considered eating there, then asked for a lunch to take with him. It wouldn't be as much fun as he'd anticipated that morning, when he'd hoped to eat a picnic dinner with Vicki. Still, on such a day as this he'd enjoy eating out of doors.

He climbed again, away from the road, pointing toward the top. His respect for Zeb Clockman was growing at each step. This had been a mountain to prospect; it was a task merely to climb.

He was growing hungry, but he wanted to get a real view before he sat down to enjoy it. He pulled himself over a cliff, using hands as well as feet, and halted.

Vicki was standing on a sort of pinnacle, gazing out at the wide view unfolded below. She turned and saw him, and her face lit up like the sun following a storm.

"King!" she exclaimed, and there was both surprise and welcome in the word.

King goggled. There was no sign of DeQuille.

"Angel on the mountain top!" he breathed. "They named this place wrong!"

Color rushed to her face, and the dimple was back in her cheek.

"Which is the Blarney stone, on the way up?" she asked. "I'd like to find it myself!"

"Sure, I wouldn't know," he confessed. "But when I

see you the words come natural. You climbed here alone?"

If she detected an emphasis on the last word, she gave no sign; she only nodded.

"Yes. I wanted to get some pictures—" She glanced at the big camera in its case, which she had temporarily laid aside. "And I like to climb, especially in country which is just as God made it, before man has spoiled it." She made a small face. "The only trouble is that I forgot to bring a lunch."

"That's no trouble, but perfect," King assured her. "I got some at Charley's, and he put up enough for half a dozen hungry men—though it'll likely be about right for the two of us, the way I feel now. I tried to find you this morning, to ask if you'd like to come along on a hike."

He spread out the lunch, and they fell to. She said nothing about the morning, and he did not press the subject. It was obvious that she hadn't gone far with DeQuille. She was there, and so was he, and that was all that mattered.

Replete, they lay and gazed, until finally she roused.

"Shouldn't we be starting back? It's heavenly here—but going down is usually tougher than climbing, and it would be an awful trail in the dark."

"I guess you're right," he conceded. "But I thought you wanted to take some pictures first."

Vicki hesitated, then nodded.

"Maybe I'd better. I've been so enthralled by the view, the food and the company that I forgot all about working." She unstrapped the camera, turned and gravely held it, gazing out at the view, then back at the instrument, frowning intently. She pressed a release, and repeated the process. King watched, smiling; then his attention sharpened. Finally he faced her, grinning.

"I'll bet those'll be lovely pictures," he observed. "Such a fine view."

"I'll bet they will, too," she agreed. "It's really breath-taking."

"Yeah. But don't you use plates in your camera, or shift them around, or anything like that? Kind of a new sort of camera, isn't it, where all you have to do is press the button and nothing else?"

Vicki looked quickly at him, her face scarlet. Then, seeing the tenderness behind the laughter in his eyes, she nodded soberly.

"You saved my life the other day, King," she said, "the first time we met. So I can trust you. That was only a blind—an excuse for coming out to this country and looking around. I've never used a camera or taken a picture in my life. What are plates? Aren't they dishes?"

"Well, some are," King conceded. "But photo plates are pieces of glass with emulsion on them, and when the light strikes through the lens of the camera, it acts on the emulsion to make a picture. I'm no expert, but I couldn't help noticing that much."

"I bought this camera second-hand, but nobody told me about plates, and I didn't think to ask," she confessed. "I suppose you think I'm pretty dumb—and rather terrible."

"Do you want me to tell you what I really think of you?" he asked eagerly. "Because it's a topic on which I could wax eloquent—"

"Then don't—not now." She colored, turning hastily away. "I know I'm dumb. But I had to do it this way. I suppose you're wondering now what I am doing here, aren't you?"

"More or less," King acknowledged. "But you don't need to tell me unless you want to. I'd take you on faith to the end of the world, Vicki. Anything you want to do is all right with me."

"Well, I'm no photographer or newspaperwoman," she conceded. "Actually, I'm out here to try to find out something about the mines—why they don't pay a profit, instead of losing money. You see, the owner is a friend of mine. And he's suspicious that something isn't as it should be. But if he came himself, then it might be hard to find what was wrong, if something is. It could be more or less covered up, you see. So we thought that maybe I could look around a little—" She stopped uncertainly.

"You'll need a camera eye that's wide open." King nodded. "I think you're right. I've a hunch there's something screwy here, too. I don't know what—but I do get that impression."

"So do I, and mine has been growing ever since I came to the camp," Vicki agreed. "King, will you help me? If we both keep our eyes open, maybe we can discover something. And I'm such a tenderfoot—I don't even know how to use a camera—"

"Maybe you don't know that, but you do know how to use your head," he said gravely. "We'll get some plates, so you can make a good showing, and as you say, we'll keep our eyes open. I'll like that—being partners with you, Vicki."

"I'll like it, too," she agreed. "I was scared before— frightened that it was too big a job for me. Now I know we'll get somewhere!"

Descending the hill was no longer a chore. As they neared the road, King halted reluctantly.

"Here's where you take the low road and me the high," he said. "It may be better if we aren't seen coming down together. Somebody might get suspicious. If what we both suspect is true, we'll find this hill has the right name, and we'd better watch our step!"

6.

Vicki had gone less than a quarter of a mile when DeQuille appeared unexpectedly.

"Have a nice time?" he asked. "Sorry I couldn't go along with you."

The words were casual, but something in the tone was too smooth, like the purr of a well-fed cat. De-Quille had come to her that morning and declared frankly that he'd like an opportunity to get better acquainted; he had suggested that perhaps they could go somewhere on a picnic. Whatever she might like, he was at her service.

Vicki had said neither yes nor no. There had been the tacit implication that he might accompany her if he wished. But DeQuille had suddenly remembered something else that he had to do—a forgotten errand which would take him out of town in the opposite direction. It had been almost too abrupt, but at the time she had felt only a sense of relief. Crumbs of information might drop from his lips, but as in the case of a hen picking corn from the mud, the muck would spoil it.

Now he was beside her, and she had the conviction that he had spent the day spying, and not in the opposite direction from town. His turning up there was too fortuitous; and he plainly didn't care if she knew it.

"Get a lot of good pictures?" he asked. "I've a hobby —taking pictures and developing them. It saves a lot of time. I'll develop your plates if you like."

"I'll keep your offer in mind," Vicki agreed. A cool wind blew down from the heights. Perhaps it was that which made her shiver.

DeQuille accompanied her back to the boarding house, exerting himself to be pleasant. He had a feeling that he'd gone too far, turning up as he had, allowing her to guess that he'd been spying. Usually he didn't bungle in such fashion, but he'd been in the grip of jealousy. She had been spending the day with Coleman, and DeQuille was fast coming to hate Coleman with an intensity such as he'd bestowed upon no other man.

Leaving the supper table, DeQuille went outside, but he walked slowly, uncertain of his next move. He should report to Apperson, for it was the foreman who paid his wages, and he was certain that Bart would be interested in what he had to tell.

But there were other angles to what went on at Helltop, other strings to his bow. Apperson would receive the information, but if some of it could be turned to his own ends, DeQuille was not adverse to doing that.

He heard a door open in the gloom ahead, saw a man outlined briefly before it closed, and started to quicken his steps. A word with Yount might be profitable.

Again he slowed at a new thought. He would see Yount, but it might work better if he had a word with Wilma first. Now was a good opportunity, since Yount was heading for Pete's Place. The mine foreman had taken to hanging out at the saloon increasingly in the evening, instead of spending time at home.

DeQuille reached the door and knocked lightly, hesitantly. He smiled to himself as the door opened and he caught the eagerness in Wilma's face before she recognized him.

"Were you expecting Coleman?" he asked smoothly, then, before she could answer, inserted his foot in the doorway. "It might be to our mutual advantage to have a little talk," he suggested.

Wilma stared at him, her eyes as bright and malignant as those of a hunting owl. She was under no illusions regarding this man, whom she thoroughly despised. In her eyes he was the lowest creature in the camp, a spy for Apperson. But for that very reason it might be expedient to treat him politely.

"Come on in, if you like," she agreed, and yawned

elaborately, "though I can't think what you mean."

"I suspect you know," DeQuille retorted, closing the door behind him. He smiled aggravatingly. "You hoped it was Coleman when you heard me knock, didn't you?"

"Coleman? Hoped? Why should I be interested in him, one way or the other? Someone knocked, I answered, and there you were."

"Have it your own way." DeQuille shrugged, helping himself to a chair. "I got the impression the other night that you rather liked the fellow."

"I used to know him, so I asked him in for a cup of coffee. What would you expect?"

"That, of course—oh, certainly that." DeQuille smirked. "And I've no advice as to who you see or at what hours. But I thought you might be able to use a friend. Maybe we could work together. Of course, if you're not interested—"

There was a silence while Wilma studied him and considered. She did not pretend to misunderstand. This was blackmail. King had incurred Apperson's dislike, but for some reason or other, Apperson was not firing him out of hand, sending him packing from the camp. Either his displeasure was too deep to be so easily satisfied, or else he was afraid of King.

DeQuille made it his business to know what was going on in the camp. He had the instincts of a ferret,

which was what made him valuable to Apperson. She
suspected that he knew a great deal which he kept to
himself, using it to his own rather than to Apperson's
advantage. Such information, for instance, as that she
had been seeing a lot of Apperson lately, however
secretly their meetings had been arranged.

"Just what is it you want?" she asked tightly.

"You despise me because I'm a spy—but I know a
lot." DeQuille shrugged. "I'd like to know more—and
you could learn a lot from both those men—some things
which I might find useful. If you'd care to co-operate—"

Wilma had a sudden sense of fear, a sensation of
skating on dangerously thin ice. It could be perilous to
refuse, but it might as easily be fatal to accede. She came
to her feet with an anger which was not simulated.

"Get out!" she blazed. "I don't know what you're
trying to suggest, but if you think I'd have anything to
do with you, you're crazy! I may be foolish, but I'm not
a fool!"

DeQuille wouldn't be deceived by an appearance of
righteous indignation, and he might turn spiteful. But it
was the safest course. Besides, she had certain inhibitions
where Coleman was concerned.

There was no doubt as to how DeQuille felt about
King; he hated him, and would do anything in his
power to destroy him. King had rebuffed her, but if she
disliked him, that was personal. There was in her a

streak of decency, and she couldn't bring herself to betray King to a man such as DeQuille.

And in any case, DeQuille would only use her, instead of protecting her interests. If he had any loyalty, which she doubted, it was to Apperson. Certainly he'd be no ally.

DeQuille bowed mockingly. He stepped out as she flung open the door, not ill-pleased with the results of the talk, and heard the slam of the door as darkness closed around him. Then, faint but distinct, there was another tiny sound. He stood unmoving, trying to place it, to think what it could have been. It had come from outside, after the closing of the door.

It must have been something falling on the planks of the walk. The door of the Yount house was set flush against the sidewalk. It could have been the door key, jarred loose by the ferocity of the slam. But that should have been on the inside of the lock—

The light was poor, but DeQuille's eyes had long training in the dark, and he was aided by a small gleam. He reached and picked up an object, a ring. He'd seen it before—Wilma's wedding band. For a moment he was puzzled.

It could hardly have popped off her finger, even at so vehement a gesture. That would be out of the question. So it must have been off already, perhaps carried loosely in a pocket. If there had been a small hole—

He remembered that it hadn't been on her finger. That had been bare, though at the moment he hadn't attached any significance to the fact. Smiling with satisfaction, DeQuille went on. He'd have that talk with Yount now.

There had been an interval of several warm, sunny days, but the weather was changing. King saw that when he awoke the next morning. Along with Moon and the rest of their crew, he had found living accommodations in the only shack which had stood untenanted in the overcrowded camp. It had remained untaken because it was so poor.

It had been intenanted, but it was a cabin. They had chinked the cracks, nailed tar-paper inside and out, and built bunks. That made it livable. Still, it was a relief to get to Maggie's and a hot breakfast.

The sky was overcast, and a wind whistled from the west, veering toward the north. As King drove up the mountain, still in the half-darkness, the wind strengthened. It whipped exposed shoulders of the hill like an ice-coated blacksnake, and toward the summit it attained near-gale ferocity. The temperature was at least thirty degrees colder than at the foot of the hill, equally as much below yesterday's mark.

As on their first day, other wagons were ahead. King sat hunched and shivering, waiting his turn at the chute, while the big horses stomped impatiently. They were sharp-shod now, but there was ice in the wind.

Six wagons had been loaded when there came a delay. The word came back. Something had gone wrong, and the ore wasn't coming up as fast as usual. The chute was empty. There would be no more for several hours.

It was not an unusual occurrence, but on such a morning it was unpleasant. They couldn't afford to return to the foot of the hill, then come back. The ten-mile round trip would probably use up all the time, keeping them constantly on the move to no purpose. But there was no shelter closer than the camp.

None, at least, for the men on the wagons. With the horses it was different. Prepared for such waits on cold days, King blanketed his horses, attaching feed-bags with oats. They would be comfortable. There were hitching-posts at intervals around the turn to tie them to. The men could wait in the change house.

King decided it was too good a chance to miss. Yount was coming down from the shafts to the change house. King walked up to it.

"Is there any chance of my taking a look around inside the mines while I'm waiting?" King asked. "I'd like to see what they're like, if I wouldn't be in the way."

Yount's face reddened. For a moment it seemed as if he were about to explode, as though such a request were unheard of. He took his time about answering, and his breathing became even again.

"Something caught in my throat," he said. His tone became almost cordial. "Why, no, I don't see any reason why you shouldn't take a look, if you like. You may have to wait a little while, though, before you can go down. Things are in sort of a mess. I'll have one of the boys guide you as soon as possible."

"Thanks," King responded. He was not quite able to make up his mind about Yount. Wilma had spoken unfavorably of him, but she had married him. Today, as on the other occasions when King had seen him, there had been an odor of whiskey on the mine foreman's breath, and what seemed like sullenness in his manner. Both of those might be accounted for by unhappiness at home. King was inclined to feel sorry for the man. He had a feeling that, under other circumstances, they might find much in common.

Yount was breathing heavily as he hurried back to the shack above the shaft of Number One Mine. He was hardly conscious of the blast of wind before he ducked into shelter. So King wanted to go down in the mines, did he? Well—he certainly had no objection to his going—deep down!

Yount had spent a night in purgatory. DeQuille had shown him the ring and turned it over to him. It was in Yount's pocket now. DeQuille had explained that he'd stopped at the house to see if Yount was there, and had given a not too garbled version of how he'd come into possession of the ring.

At first Yount had been inclined to go back and fling the ring in Wilma's face, making violent accusations. He was headlong by nature, rather than devious. But the other things which DeQuille had told him, veiled suggestions and insinuations linking Wilma's name with Coleman's, had changed his mind.

Yount loved his wife. Sometimes, in moments of introspection, he wondered why he continued to do so. He had long since discovered that she had married him only because she had supposed that he had some money and would make a lot more. He'd never sought to give that impression, but somehow she had gotten it.

Her disillusion, like his own, had been great. She had made it plain on many occasions that now she had only contempt for him.

He'd been aware for some time that she was two-timing him, that she continued to stay with him only because he was a meal ticket until she could get something better. The knowledge should have made him hate her. Instead, it had been like a knife thrust deeper into a raw wound. He was a fool, but he still loved her, still wanted her, on any terms. And he was insanely jealous.

Yount saw no reason to doubt what DeQuille told

him. He knew the real nature of DeQuille's work as a snooper for the big boss. DeQuille would know what he was talking about.

A combination of whiskey and jealousy had made Yount devious. He had decided to wait for a favorable opportunity, then take action.

He hadn't expected the chance to come so soon, but he was ready for it. A man who would steal another man's wife deserved no pity. What he would do to Coleman would hurt Wilma at the same time. He would have a full, fitting revenge.

Out of the blast of wind, Yount paused, shivering, partly from the cold, but more from a sick feeling of revulsion. He wasn't accustomed to doing things in such fashion, striking like a coward. But it was the only way. If he clashed openly with the big man, then, whoever won, Wilma would know all about it, and she would probably retaliate by leaving him for Coleman. This way, she could never do that—and fool that he was, he couldn't bear to lose her.

Yount opened a cupboard and reached a half-empty flask of whiskey. Tipping it, he drank gustily. The shivering stopped, and his mind became as cold as his throat was hot. After all, there was only one way to treat a skunk.

Except for himself, the shed above Number I was empty. There were three mines working, three shafts on the hilltop, all spewing their ores into the one chute which fed the wagons. Each shaft descended straight down into the hill. Side-tunnels branched off at intervals. There was a big, interconnected world, over which Yount presided.

From Number 1, at the two-hundred-foot depth, a side-tunnel led off, following the vein of ore. Farther on, it made connection with Mine 3. For some time now, all ore had been taken out through Mine 3, which was at a lower level. That did away with the necessity of hoisting it. But workmen still ascended and descended in the original shaft of Number 1.

A utility elevator carried them up and down. It operated on cables attached to overhead pulleys, on the simplest possible principle. Compressed air from a power plant furnished the motive power.

The elevator was no more than a floor of heavy planking, enclosed by a three-foot railing with a gate. It filled the square shaft to within a few inches on all sides. In this, swaying uneasily, the men rode up and down. Since the shaft was always in pitch darkness except for the feeble glow of their lamps, they had no fear of the depths.

The trouble which had halted operations was in Mine 2. All the crew from number 1 had been shifted there to clear up the difficulty, so that Number 1 shaft was temporarily empty. Yount worked swiftly.

A grimy miner, a stranger to King, approached him where he waited at the change house.

"The boss says you want to go down in Number 1 and have a look," he said. "Come along. I'll show you around."

He led the way, climbing the steep, winding path up the hill, around great rocks, in a breathless ascent, until the shed above Number 1 was reached. Inside, he gave King a head lamp, helping him to adjust it and get it alight. It was a small lantern with reflector, using kerosene for fuel. There was a bigger lantern in the elevator. In the darkness, the lights were like lonesome fireflies in the vast sweep of a prairie night. The guide motioned for him to step through the gate.

"Get on," he instructed. "It's kind of shaky when you step on, but it's safe enough."

King obeyed. His guide paused to throw a switch and started to follow, but something went wrong before he could do so. King heard the snap as the elevator started to move, a whistling, rasping sound made by a giant cable snaking suddenly along a screaming pulley wheel, whipping at dizzy speed.

The platform beneath his feet lurched wildly, one side tipping sharply; then it started to drop in a terrifying plunge. King had a glimpse of the guide's white, startled face; then it was out of sight, appearing to shoot upward as the big cage plummeted into the darkness.

7.

King staggered at the first sickening lurch, almost thrown off his feet. In the same instant he realized what had occurred. One of the cables had parted, and the opposite cable, instead of locking and holding, was slipping, giving way without resistance. The cage was commencing an unchecked drop. By the time it crashed at the bottom of the shaft, it would be kindling wood, and anyone who rode it down would be jelly—even his bones.

There was no time for conscious thought or planning. The plunge had started fast, and it would accelerate at tremendous speed. But there was an instant before the dropping cage gathered momentum. In that moment, King had a look at the side. His head was poised to see squarely, and he shone the light of his lamp into an opening. An instant later he was jumping, still without conscious volition, in an instinctive reaction of self-preservation.

The opening was a side-shaft which had been started and quickly abandoned. It was no larger than a small-sized room beside the main shaft. But there it was, and it offered a chance.

The lurching floor of the cage was in his favor. It gave him a lift and heave. The rail of the cage and the cage itself dropped away and he found himself clawing forward in sudden and complete darkness. His lamp had gone out.

His arms reached the floor of the side-room, but his legs dangled over space. Heaving desperately, he climbed and crawled forward, panting from terror more than from the effort. A thunderous crash shook the hill, booming back up the shaft. Something writhed and hissed like a great snake in its death convulsions—the broken cable, settling above the wreckage of the cage. Then there was silence.

The gloom above lightened faintly, and a voice exclaimed hoarsely—the horrified voice of his guide.

"God Almighty!" he said.

Yount's voice came, sharp and edgy. "What the devil's happened?"

"You can see." The guide was obviously shaken. "Cable busted, seems like. He'd just stepped on the car, and I threw the switch and was startin' to get on when it happened. It just fell away from me—I almost tumbled into the hole 'fore I could jerk back. The poor devil!" he added softly.

"Funny how such a thing could happen," Yount muttered, and now his own voice was shaken. "Well, it's done now. He wouldn't have a chance."

"I'm down here," he called, and could picture the consternation which his voice must rouse in those who were sure that he was a part of the wreckage. "Here in the side-shaft right below you. How about throwing me a rope?"

There was a moment's strained silence, broken by the sound of other men coming into the room above, attracted by the crash. Then the guide's voice answered uncertainly:

"You're alive?"

"Sure I'm alive," King agreed. "I jumped. Now how about a rope?"

It was quickly forthcoming, lowered by several willing hands which quickly hoisted him up. The miners regarded him, exclaiming, still hardly believing that he could have escaped.

"Man, it's a miracle to see you!" Hard-Rock Baker assured him. "I wouldn't have believed it. But it's glad I am that you're here!"

"I'm rather glad of it myself," King agreed. "It's dark down there."

"I sure don't know what happened to that cable." The guide sighed, mopping at his face with a stained bandana. "The car was workin' fine just a little while ago."

"Better take a look at it and see what did go wrong," King suggested, and made his way outside again, pausing to gulp in lungfuls of the sharp air. Yount, he noticed, had already found some errand to take him elsewhere.

He'd have given a lot for an opportunity to examine the broken cable himself. It would probably show the marks of a saw. But if what he suspected was correct, Yount would keep everybody out of Number 1 until he'd retrieved that piece of cable himself.

King had scarcely returned to his wagon and seen to the comfort of his horses when the word came. Due to the new accident, the wreckage which had to be cleared, and the fact that a new elevator had to be installed, there would be no more ore to haul that day, and probably the next.

That meant more missed wages. The narrow margin of profit which he and Moon had counted on would be wiped out, their work for nothing, unless—

After reaching town and stabling his team, he returned for dinner, and was disappointed to find Vicki absent. Momentarily he hesitated, considering. If there was danger for him, might there not also be peril for her, trying to pry into secrets which the big boss obviously wanted to keep hidden? But it seemed unlikely, at least at this stage of the game. They had no reason to suspect her, and they were concentrating their worry and dislike on him. King grinned. That was fine. He'd rather be their target than have them pick on Vicki.

The storm still held off, but was ever more threatening. As he secured a horse and started to ride out of town, snow began to fall. That suited him. It would cloak his movements and cover his trail, in case he was still being watched as closely as on Sunday. Then he'd had nothing more serious in mind than to inquire about wagons which had never come.

It was a score of miles to the county seat, off on a road he hadn't taken before. The wind had died, and the air warmed somewhat as the snow continued to fall.

King reached his destination in mid-afternoon. The offices of the courthouse were gloomy despite the lights which burned, and the office of the recorder was deserted save for a clerk. He obligingly helped King with maps and information, and having located what he had in mind, King hid his elation. The land at the base of Helltop, back along the canyon, was open to settlement or homesteading. The clerk could scarcely hide his surprise that anyone should be interested in such ground, where a goat would be hard put to it to exist. But he filled out the forms, and presently King had a promissory lease from Uncle Sam for the canyon where the waste from the mines had spilled.

To make doubly sure of his rights, he filed on a mineral claim as well, which would compass the whole pile of waste. It was above, rather than below ground, and had been discarded, but it was better to be safe than sorry.

Technically, King had not yet set his stakes or affixed a location notice, but nobody would know the difference until he had it attended to. It was night when he returned to Silverhill, but he kept on without stopping, finally reaching his own ground. There, working painfully in storm and darkness, he made sure of possession by setting the stakes and writing out the location notice to the claim.

He might be whistling in the dark. Perhaps there was no more value to that vast pile of waste than the two foremen and their experts believed. But if his hunch was correct, they could be in for some surprises.

Apperson possessed one requisite of a good foreman. During working hours he was generally on the job, quickly at hand when anything went wrong. King had scarcely left the hilltop when Apperson arrived at the scene of the crash.

He promptly took charge, going down on a rope ladder to have a look at the smashed elevator, since the wreckage had blocked the shaft leading to the other mines. Making the trip required courage; he knew how far it was to the bottom. A rope ladder was tricky and unpleasant to descend, worse to climb back up. But no one had ever accused Apperson of lack of nerve.

Yount descended after him, looking around grimly in the scant light of their head lamps. When Apperson picked up an end of the broken cable and studied it, he waited with a show of stoicism which he was far from feeling. Inwardly he was screwed tight, feeling a strong revulsion against his murderous impulse of earlier in the day. He was like a dishrag wrung dry— wrung dry of dirty water.

Apperson's face was without expression, but when he turned there was a quizzical light in his eyes.

"You say Coleman was on the cage when it started to drop?" he asked.

Yount had not said that. Others had explained to Apperson. But he nodded.

"That's what I understand."

"And he jumped for that old side-tunnel and saved himself! That man has the devil's own luck."

"It was luck, all right," Yount conceded.

"Luck beyond what a man has any right to count on," Apperson agreed. He made no reference to the saw marks, but it came to Yount that he was not displeased. Yount, climbing back up to daylight, wished he could say as much for himself. He was conscious of a growing relief that his trick had failed. But with it remained the feeling that he had stepped into a mudhole and sunk far deeper than he had anticipated—and that the mud was blacker, dirtier, than anything he'd ever known before.

Word came the next morning. No hauling for the wagons that day. Moon's face, in the early dawn, was as gray as the day.

"Looks like the jinx has followed us here, King." He sighed. "Either there's a hex on this camp, or on us. I had the notion that the mines were big business, makin' a lot of money. But I've been lookin' around since we came, and that ain't no more'n a false front. Way they're bein' run, they're apt to go busted and have to shut down. And everybody here is teeterin' on the edge of ruin right now.

"Take Maggie," he went on. "With us, she's feedin' thirty men three meals a day. Workin' hard to do it, and you'd say she ought to be makin' money. Which ain't the case. The more she feeds, and the longer, the worse off she is."

"You mean she's chargin' too low a price?"

"Not that, exactly. She's chargin' what seems to her to be fair, when wages are so low. Ordinary, she could make it. But with all the shut-downs, days when men don't make anything, and with some of them drinkin' up their wages 'fore they pay their board bill—she's so kind-hearted that she's been carryin' some of 'em for months, and the longer things go on, the worse it gets."

"That's bad," King acknowledged. "We'll pay our own bills, at least."

"Yeah—but for how long? Gosh blame it, King, when I saw Maggie again, after all these years—" Moon colored like a boy. "Well, I got notions that I thought I'd long forgot. Felt like a kid again, and set to makin' big plans. But if we can't even break even up here, to say nothin' of gettin' a grubstake—" He spread his hands. "She's got troubles enough without me addin' to them, let alone shoulderin' 'em," he finished.

King clapped him on the back.

"Buck up," he advised. "We aren't licked yet. In fact, I've a hunch this is going to turn out to be a good winter."

He hoped he was right, as he stepped outside and turned down the street. He'd lifted Moon's spirits, but it might be an empty gesture. King scanned the sky. It was still overcast, and more snow was beginning to filter out of the murky gray. Overnight it had turned much colder. There was a crackling quality to the air. It must be close to zero. He shivered, thinking of the ride ahead.

The stableman thought of the same thing when King

asked for a horse.

"Be mighty cold ridin' today," he suggested. "Tell you what. Why don't you take a team and buggy? I've got a pair of good trotters there, just layin' around and eatin' themselves sick. A run'll do them good. And there's curtains for the buggy, and a buffalo robe. I won't charge you any more than for a saddle horse."

King accepted gratefully. The buggy was a single-seater, but with the top up and the curtains adjusted, much of the cold would be kept out. The isinglass in the curtains was cracked and yellowed, but there was considerable protection. Wrapped in a heavy robe, he was snug enough.

He reflected briefly. He had no way of knowing whether or not he had been watched or followed the day before, but certainly a close watch had been kept on his movements the previous Sunday, when they had been innocent enough. After yesterday, he was probably the object of increased curiosity, none of it friendly. Swinging in at the hitch-rail, he tied the team and entered Pete's Place.

At that chill morning hour, the saloon was empty except for the bartender, the same man to whom he had given the revolvers that he had taken from his assailants at Tenbrooke. He'd left them with instructions to return them if they were claimed.

"Has anybody called for them?" he asked. The bartender, busily polishing the big mirror, shook his head.

"Yes—and no," he said. "One feller made some kind of cautious inquiries, and I figured it was those guns he was hintin' at. But then he's always tryin' to find out things. So I acted dumb, and he didn't pursue the subject by comin' right out. Kind of coy."

"So you still have the guns?"

"I still do."

"In that case, I think I'll borrow one back," King suggested. It was promptly forthcoming. The bartender eyed him obliquely.

"I heard how you caught a whiff of brimstone yesterday," he remarked, "when that mine cage dropped with you. Man, you got luck—but I'd sure pack a gun regular, was I you, and watch your step."

"That might be good advice," King agreed. "You didn't happen to know the gent who was pesticatin' you with those question?"

"I could have been wrong as to what he had in mind," the bartender conceded carefully. "But in any case he's what you'd call a snooper. Without namin' no names, mebby that'll answer your question."

"Why, maybe it will—and thanks," King agreed, and went back to the buggy. So it had been DeQuille who had asked. He wasn't surprised.

The horses stepped out briskly against the chill of the day, their breath sending out frosty clouds as they ran. It was not a comfortable ride. The deep ruts cut by his own and other wagons when there had been rain and mud had not been filled or smoothed by the ensuing traffic. Snow had filled them now, but when the buggy wheels dropped in, the light vehicle slewed and swerved. There were icy spots where it required a firm hand on the reins to steady the horses, sharp-shod though they were. But this was easy, compared with what the road off Helltop would be a little later.

A couple of hours of driving brought him to Rock Camp, even more cheerless in the falling snow than it had looked before. The shacks crowded the hill, remnants of a gold rush which had soon petered out. Now there seemed no reason for the existence of the town. Probably a few old-timers clung to the hope which ever blossoms in the heart of a true prospector: that some day a big strike would reward their faith.

There was no livery barn in the town, but he found an old man who had an empty barn, and stabled the horses against the cold. Then he walked to Van Cleeve's Assay Office. He had made sure that there was none in Silverhill, none even at the country seat. H. Van Cleeve, like others, had come there in the heyday of bright hopes, and had remained.

A stove glowed warmly in the one-room shack, and Van Cleeve looked up as King entered. He was a small, bright-eyed man, with a habit of cocking his head to the side and squinting obliquely. "Howdy," he said briefly, and waited.

King emptied samples from a sack onto the scarred counter. Behind the desk were the tools of Van Cleeve's trade—enough to do the work, but no more.

"I'm curious about these specimens," King explained. "Could you run a test on them now and set my mind at rest?"

Van Cleeve squinted at one of the chunks of ore.

"In a hurry?"

"Sort of. I'd like it if you could do it now."

"Guess I can manage. Ain't been very busy lately. Take a few hours."

"I'll stick around, then," King said cheerfully. "Nothing else to do, and it's too cold a day to be on the road for nothing."

The assayer grunted, but set to work. King lingered a few minutes to watch. From the way Van Cleeve went about it, it was easy to tell that he knew what he was doing. King was in a position to judge, for in the course of many jobs across the years, he'd once assisted in an assay office in the gold country for several weeks. Since Van Cleeve remained uncommunicative, he went back out.

Three or four inches of fresh snow had fallen, but now it was slackening. There was the promise of a break in the clouds, but such sun as might shine today would hold little heat. King killed time as best he could, not an easy task in a camp where industry had ground to a dead stop. He got something to eat with the old man who had offered his barn. The fare was hardtack, a slab of thick boiled beans spooned from a kettle and heated, and coffee strong enough to stand by itself.

Fortified, King wandered about awhile, then returned to the assay office. Van Cleeve appeared to have finished his tests. He was working laboriously on the report, his face screwed up as he clutched a broken stub of pencil. He looked up.

"You didn't give me your name.

"Coleman," King said. "Lynn Coleman."

Van Cleeve wrote it down. Then he sighed and shoved the paper forward.

"That'll be five dollars," he said. "Sorry I can't give you good news to pay for it."

"It's not a good report, then?" King kept his voice impersonal, reminding himself that he hadn't expected too much. Van Cleeve shrugged.

"Most stuff that folks bring me is worthless," he said. "It looks like yours could have come right off the dump. All it is is trash."

8

The day had begun gray, and it became more depressing as it wore on. Wilma had already spent one winter at the camp, and it had been her fervent hope that she would not have to spend another. Here in the Washoes it could turn bleakly cold, but it was the isolation which she hated. There was nothing in the town, even in summer. It was remote from a railroad, so even traveling theatrical troupes passed it by.

A dozen times she passed her nose to the window pane, staring disconsolately at the sidewalk, which was all that was visible through the storm. She strained her ears as footsteps made an occasional muffled clomp up to the door and past—always past. On such a day, King might come again, though in her heart she knew that he would not. It was growing as cold as the weather.

Despite her conviction, she started eagerly when a knock sounded and hastened to throw the door open. Her face changed when she recognized her caller. Bart

Apperson stepped inside quickly, shaking snow from his heavy coat, looking like an oversized wooden idol. He reached in an automatic gesture to take her in his arms, but she avoided him without appearing to do so by taking the coat as it slipped from his shoulders.

Neither of them felt the need for explanations. Each knew that Yount was busy on the hill, and would be there for the remainder of the day. Apperson had never before ventured to come to the house by daylight, but with the storm so thick, he was not apt to be noticed.

"You don't seem very happy to see me," he observed, and jealousy burred his tones. "What's this I've been hearing about Coleman being an old flame of yours?"

It would be useless to deny it. DeQuille would have carried the report, garbled and enlarged because of her rebuff. Wilma shrugged.

"You haven't seemed to have any time for me lately," she pointed out. "Apparently I'm no more than a toy, a convenience, when you've nothing better to do."

Her attempt to place him on the defensive partially succeeded. Apperson flushed.

"That's not so, and you know it," he protested. "There've been a lot of things to keep me busier than usual lately, and besides, I can't barge in here any time I think of it. But you're dodging my question."

Wilma allowed herself to be partly mollified. "I'm not dodging it," she said. "Coleman's nothing to me.

Maybe he was once—but not enough to make me want him then, so why should I now? Your spy is mad because Coleman has treated him a little roughly—and I don't like DeQuille any better than he does!"

Apperson colored again at this reference to DeQuille. The man was an object of general contempt and dislike, but he was often useful. Nonetheless, his reports might be tinted by spite.

"We won't worry about him." He shrugged. "I just wanted to make sure that Coleman doesn't mean anything to you. That's important, because I think he's here as a spy himself. I figure the company has hired him. Certainly he's sticking his nose into everything—and I may have to take steps. So I have to know where you stand."

Wilma's face remained carefully blank. There had been many occasions when it had been necessary to mask her emotions. Her quick surge of apprehension told her what she had been trying to deny—that she was concerned where King was involved. Had that falling elevator at the mine been more than an accident—an attempt to kill him?

"Did you try to take steps with the mine cage?" she asked.

"That? No. It was your husband who sawed the cable almost in two. I didn't know anything about it until afterward." His eyes sharpened at the recollection.

"*He* must have figured that he had some reason for jealousy!"

Panic tore like claws, but only for a moment. Beneath a baby-like façade, she had a coolly objective mind.

"Yount has guessed that there's been another man for quite a while." She shrugged. "If he thought it was you—" She allowed that suggestion to dangle. "He must have jumped to conclusions—DeQuille again." Suddenly she became pleading, urgent, her hands on his shoulders.

"But we can't go on this way, Bart. Not any longer. Yount is suspicious, and he's dangerous! Besides, I'm sick of all this—of being cooped up in this camp, away from everything that makes life worth-while. You promised me that we'd get out where people move, where the lights are soft instead of only dim!"

"That's why I'm here," Apperson told her. "What do you think I've been working at lately? The only trouble is that if that young fool back East is getting suspicious, I'll have to move faster. I've made arrangements for backing, so that when the company is bankrupt I can get control for a song. It shouldn't take long now. Then—you name it, and we'll have it! New York, Paris, Vienna—anywhere."

Wilma's eyes grew bright. "That's the sort of talk I've been waiting to hear," she replied. "What do you want me to do?"

"I only want to be sure that you won't do anything," Apperson warned. Infatuated he might be, but she had long since discovered that he was no fool. "Matters are going to be in pretty delicate balance for a while, and if Coleman is what I suspect, he could be dangerous. I don't want an enemy in my own camp, someone carrying tales or sticking a knife in my back. Do you understand?"

Wilma looked hurt.

"If that's all the trust you have in me—"

"I'm fool enough to be crazy about you, but not crazy enough to be a fool," Apperson retorted. "Stick along with me, and you'll wear diamonds. I think your self-interest should be enough to show you how to behave. But I have to be sure at a time like this. You stick with me, and you won't regret it. But double-cross me, and I'll twist that pretty neck of yours!"

King ambled across to the barn, then paused inside the door to study the report. According to the assay, there were traces of silver, but not in sufficient quantities to be profitable. There was a little gold—just enough to excite a tenderfoot, but, as Van Cleeve had said, worthless.

It looked as if the mine foreman knew what he was about when so much stuff was dumped as waste. And yet—

There had been a curious glitter in the eyes of Van Cleeve when King had returned, an air of excitement which the little man could not quite hide.

There was a sound of wheels, and King turned, peering through a crack in the siding. Another buggy, much like his own, was going past, heading out of town in the direction of Silverhill, traveling at a fast trot. King had only a glimpse, but the driver looked like Van Cleeve.

It was starting to snow again, the clouds thickening after an abortive break. If anything, it was colder than before. King let himself out, closing the barn door, and headed back for the assay office. Standing well off by itself, it was hidden by the storm. The door was closed but not locked. After a moment, King let himself in.

DeQuille dragged himself wearily into town. Following his earlier report, Apperson had given him a single assignment: to keep an eye on Coleman. It was proving a tougher job than anything DeQuille had worked at up till now.

Apperson listened with strained attention as DeQuille gave his report.

"I lost him for a while yesterday," he confessed. "It was snowing hard. But I picked up his trial again. He went to the county seat."

"The county seat?" Apperson ejaculated. "What the

blazes would he want there?"

"That's what I asked myself. And it seemed to me that it would have to have something to do with the courthouse. I figured maybe he wanted to talk to the county prosecutor, or maybe the sheriff." His tone was smooth, but there was a mocking glitter in his eyes.

"The sheriff?" Apperson repeated. His hands, gripping his chair arms, showed white. "What did he do?" he asked harshly.

"Like I say, that was just an idea," DeQuille explained. "It turned out he hadn't been to either place. Then I got track of him in the recorder's office."

Apperson scowled thoughtfully. "What was he up to there?"

"He filed on a homestead." At Apperson's look of amazement, he went on, "The land he filed on takes in a lot of completely worthless country, too rough to find a place to build a house on, almost. But it has all the waste from the mines, there at the end of that big canyon. Do you begin to get it?"

"It sounds as though he's crazy," Apperson grunted.

"Wait till you hear the rest. He also filed a mineral claim for that dump—just in case, I suppose, the surface rights weren't enough."

Apperson shook his head, perplexed.

"What the devil does he want that for?" he demanded. "The stuff's no good." He smiled crookedly.

"Or does he suspect where some of the waste goes, and think it's there, too?"

"I wouldn't know," DeQuille said wearily. "It sounds crazy, but I thought you'd want to know. If he's working for Clockman, why should he do all that? All I know for sure is that I've been all night getting the dope and getting back, and I'm played out. Now I'm going to bed."

"All right; you've done a good job," Apperson commended him. "But if he's crazy, I suspect it's the same way a coyote is crazy to smell out a trap. I—"

He was pacing back and forth. He halted, peering with sudden intentness from the window, then beckoned to DeQuille.

"Isn't that him in that buggy just starting out? It is," he added, as Coleman alighted from the buggy and entered Pete's Place. "Get down there, fast, and get a couple of men to watch what he does today. Get as many men as necessary, only have them keep out of his sight!"

DeQuille obeyed, returning presently.

"He's being followed," he said. "He seems to be heading back along the road that they first came here on. He might be headin' for Van Cleeve's," he added.

"That could be a good guess," Apperson agreed. He paced the room, picking at his lower lip with nervous fingers. "If that's where he's going, I've got an idea," he added. "And everything's perfect for it—snow, cold."

DeQuille waited, catching the deadly quality of the excitement which emanated from his employer.

"It's time we got him out of our hair, whatever he's up to," Apperson added. "Van Cleeve will protect my interests, and let me know what's going on. Coleman is becoming a nuisance, and he might be a menace. Now listen closely. You can miss a few more hours of sleep, for this is important. And this time, we can't afford any mistakes."

The day was growing old when King concluded his tests. It might be that he hadn't done them in orthodox fashion or as thoroughly as Van Cleeve would have, but he had satisfied himself, and excitement put a pleasurable warmth in his blood as he let himself out and moved back to the barn. There was no longer any doubt that Van Cleeve had been lying, and he could understand the excitement which had motivated the little man.

If King's theory was correct, the vein of silver was pinching out. Now they were running increasingly into the worthless stuff—worthless, if you were after silver, and only silver.

Van Cleeve's excitement would be more than matched when he made his report to Apperson. But if King's judgment was correct, no word of it would be made public or sent back to the owner of the mines.

King hitched up his team and set out on the return journey. It would be dark by the time he reached Silverhill, as it had been that first day. Perhaps it was as well. He wouldn't be so easy to keep track of in the night and storm.

The cold was crackling, intense. King glimpsed the creek which ran beside the road. It came tumbling out of the hills, but now it was freezing, coated by snow. It was scenic, but very cold.

Just ahead the road curved, climbing steeply. The horses shied, snorting. King checked them warily. After a moment he heard a sound, faint, difficult to place. It was something like the thumping made by a rabbit, only louder.

A speck of shining white, different from the snow, caught his eyes. It was a broken sapling, at the lower side of the road, growing up from below. Here the road not only curved as it climbed, but the wagons had worn it so that it sloped treacherously to the brink, doubly hazardous under the fresh coat of snow. It looked as if something had slid off there, breaking the tree as it crashed down.

Backing his own team, King tied the horses to another tree. To circle for a look it was necessary to go back and descend from the road, then push through a tangle of brush to reach the spot.

Nearly a hundred feet below the roadway he found what he sought. The snow had covered most sign, but some, like the broken sapling, remained. There was a buggy, lying upside down, bent and twisted. One wheel was broken, and the tongue, snapped off in the middle, stuck straight up in the air.

One horse was still in the harness, lying with its head at a grotesque angle. The snow which sifted above it no longer melted from the heat of the body.

It took longer to discover the second horse, which had lodged a few feet higher up. It had been kept from slipping lower by an outcrop of rock and a crushed clump of brush. This animal stirred as he approached, lifting its head, thumping it down again in an agony of pain and frustration. The horse was too badly injured to rise.

Last of all King discovered the man who had been driving the team. He lay unmoving, partly pinned down by the dead animal and the wreckage. Hampered by side-curtains and a heavy robe, he had been unable to extricate himself and jump when the buggy started to slide. The robe was still in a tangle about him.

King recognized Van Cleeve. He was alive, but appeared to be unconscious. The robe and the warmth of the dead horse had thus far kept him from freezing.

But he was becoming very cold, and would certainly die unless help were quickly gotten. King set his hands under Van Cleeve's arms and tugged, then paused. It would take a strong pull to drag him loose, and even the slight effort indicated that any movement might start the wreckage sliding—and in such fashion as not only to pinion but to crush him.

He did not appear to be caught too securely, and if uninjured, could possible have extricated himself. So he might not be too badly hurt. If given a chance, he might survive.

King drew his gun. The injured horse had to be put out of its misery. A slide might set it thrashing again and precipitate the crisis he hoped to avert.

The gun made a brittle sound in the sharp cold. Before the noise ebbed the horse made a final, frantic effort in its death throes. Desperation succeeded where previous attempts had failed. It heaved up, then commenced to slide straight toward Van Cleeve.

King jumped and grabbed at Van Cleeve, pulling hard. With a shock, he saw that Van Cleeve's eyes had opened and were staring into his.

Sweat popped on King's face at the effort, and still nothing happened. In another moment, they'd both be caught and crushed. Setting his teeth, he strained harder. Van Cleeve groaned; then King staggered back as something gave.

It was close. The slipping animal crashed down, and a hoof lashed as though with deliberate calculation. It grazed King's arm with a numbing impact and caught Van Cleeve alongside the head. King lost his balance and pitched backward.

Presently he was able to get Van Cleeve in his arms and carry him back to the buggy. The assayer was unconscious again, his face bruised and bloody from the final buffeting of the hoof.

Arranging the robe, King started to climb in beside him, then turned and went up the road. There had to be a reason for such an accident as had occurred. In fact, there had been too many such happenings lately to put them down as accidents.

The road was snow-covered, but there was no ice beneath the covering—at least there had been none up to that point. As he started to climb the slope, his feet went out from under him. King barely saved himself from going over the side.

Where his slide had shoved the snow aside, there was a glassy sheet of ice where none had been when he had traveled the other way.

Under the snow the road looked normal, and the marks of sliding hoofs and wheels had been covered over.

This was a trap, and he had no doubt that he, not Van Cleeve, had been the intended victim. As on other occasions, it was clear that his movements had been watched. Probably he had been seen reaching Rock

Camp and heading for the assay office.

Preparing the trap had not been difficult. A couple of men could dip buckets of water from the tumbling creek close at the side, and pour them over the road in a matter of minutes. In even less time there had been a sheet of glare ice, the water freezing as it touched the flinty earth. Afterward the snow had covered all sign.

Starting up at a brisk pace, Van Cleeve's horses had last their footing, then commenced to slide. It had worked as planned; buggy and team were unable to stop, plunging over the side to destruction.

The only hitch was that this trap had been set for him, instead of the victim it had claimed.

9.

There was a single medico in Silverhill, a man who usually found plenty to keep him busy. The mines produced nearly as many injuries as they did tons of ore. King had seen the faded sign on a building, but he did not remember where. Night was closing. The best thing would be to impose further on the good nature of Maggie Travis, take Van Cleeve there, then get the doctor.

He pulled up, jumped down and gathered the unconscious man in his arms. The door opened before he came to it, and Vicki's anxious face was revealed in the warm glow of light.

"I saw you pull up," she explained and, taking in the condition of the injured man at a glance, did not pause for questions. "This way," she added, and led the way to a bedroom. King stretched Van Cleeve on the bed.

"Where's Maggie?" King asked.

"She's out with Moon," Vicki explained. "I'm the only one home."

"I'll go for the doctor," King said. Supper was over. Vicki observed his dishevelment, the raking mark of the hoof along his sleeve, the blood from the injured man on his clothes. But she did not blanch or question him.

"I'll stay with him," she agreed.

King set off, running. He stopped impatiently as his name was called.

"King! What's your hurry? Or were you hurrying to see me—I hope?"

The provocative tone, matched by the look in Wilma's eyes, found no response in his own. He answered shortly:

"I've got to find the doctor. There's a man badly injured."

"Oh." Her tone denoted understanding but not much concern. Injured men were rather a commonplace in the camp. "Probably you'll find him at Pete's Place about now."

"Thanks." Before he could go on, she stopped him again.

"I thought we were friends, King—and this is an awfully lonesome town!"

I've been pretty busy," he said impatiently. "And I can't stop now."

"Of course not. But maybe you could take a little time after you've gotten the doctor."

"I'll try," he promised, eager to get away, and hurried on. True to her guess, Doc Patman was at a table in the rear of the saloon, relaxing over a friendly game of cards. He did not drink, but saloons served as the only clubhouses in the camp. He sighed, laid down his hand, then rose briskly as King made known his errand.

"Best hand I've drawn in a month of Sundays," he said resignedly. "I picked the wrong profession; should have buried people instead of trying to keep 'em alive. Keep a man just about as busy, but not so urgent." He retrieved his bag from behind the bar and followed King out into the night.

For the next hour, King had no time to think of Wilma. He and Vicki were both kept busy assisting the doctor, who worked in silence save for brief instructions. Finally he straightened. Van Cleeve had been cleaned up, a broken arm set, bruises treated.

"It's a wonder that he's alive," the doctor declared. "I suppose the buggy and the heavy robe padded his fall. Whether he'll stay alive is a question. He has a few broken ribs, and there may be internal injuries. He's in more or less of a coma—probably the result of that knock with the hoof. That is perhaps a good thing for the present, if it doesn't last too long. We can only wait and hope and see what develops. With good care, he may survive."

"He'll get that, Doctor," Vicki promised. Her eyes

were warm with sympathy. "I'll see that he does."

"That will make the difference, if anything can," Patman assured her. "I'll be back tomorrow. Call me sooner if it seems necessary, but I don't think it will be."

He took his departure, and Vicki bustled about to get King some supper.

He was finishing the meal when a sound sent them hurrying to the bedside. Van Cleeve was still unconscious, but he was coughing, choking on blood. One on either side of the bed, they turned him so that the blood would run out rather than down his throat, and presently the bleeding abated and he seemed more comfortable. When Maggie and Lena returned, along with Moon and Dan O'Leary, and he was able to leave, King was too weary to think of anything except bed.

By morning, the snow had recommenced. Old-timers shook their heads. Winter was coming early, with the teeth in its jaws. If this was a fair indication of what was ahead, Helltop would be no misnomer.

There was ore ready for hauling, and the rule was to move it when it was ready, with no delays permitted on account of bad roads or worse weather. If one man didn't want the job, there were always plenty of others anxious to try. *Borrasco* cracked a bitter whip.

There was no change in Van Cleeve's condition. King looked in at breakfast, then drove his wagon up the mountain in a cloud of white, following other wagons.

King picked up a load of miners, trudging ghost-like toward the crest, heads sunk deep in heavy collars, icicles covering beards and mustaches. Hard-Rock Baker commented feelingly on the job ahead for the drivers when they took the down-grade.

"This is as bad as anything I've seen in a couple of years here," he confessed. "Usually, times like this, somebody has trouble. I'm sure glad my job's inside the hill."

"You fellows are pessimists," King retorted, but found it hard to grin in the numbing cold. At the top of the hill, he waited his turn, listening to the various sounds.

He was conscious of the grating slide of ore in the chute, the quick heavy whoom as it plummeted into a wagon box. There was the fainter rasp of a car of ore, being emptied into the top of the chute and rumbling down to take its place with the supply already there. There was the rougher sound of a load of waste, dumped into the other chute, sliding much farther, then suddenly spilling into space with only a faint noise.

King heard these sounds twice, then a third time, and instinctively his head lifted from burrowing into the coat collar. Somehow there was a difference in that last sound, though he could not quite define the difference. It had been ore in the waste chute, there was no doubt of that. But some quality was not the same.

The noise remained like a buzzing bee to aggravate a corner of his mind as he drove on with his load down the mountain. The horses plodded slowly, setting their feet with heavy caution, as though aware that much depended on them. Easing along, moving with a sure instinct, they reached the bottom of the hill and a feed.

It continued to snow. Once more waiting at the top, King found himself unconsciously listening, classifying the various sounds. Again he was puzzled by the difference when some of the waste was dumped. It should all sound alike—

Word came back that there would be a temporary delay, because of trouble in Number 2 mine. The chute was empty. There would be more ore in an hour or so, but until then they'd have to wait. King blanketed his horses, then spoke to Flood.

"Keep an eye on them, will you, Mike? I've something to do for a little while."

The halt at that spot and the storm which afforded cover was too good a chance to miss. King descended cautiously from the road, for a slip into the mighty gorge could send a man tumbling as far as the waste. Since waste was shunted into a separate chute, it was still being emptied at intervals, as the noise testified.

He was around a shoulder of cliff, out of sight of the

road and a couple of hundred feet below, when another load of waste came plunging. King looked up to see it roar down the chute and plummet off into space. The rattle of its descent came back.

That had been a normal sound. Now there was a new grating sound, and again waste came sliding into view. Then there was a change. Something got in the way. The snow made it hard to see, but he knew it was a gate, erected across the chute, probably by jerking a rope from somewhere higher up. At the same time, another gate opened in the side of the chute, and the ore changed course, spilling into another chute at the side and below—*one invisible from above!*

The load went hurtling along, but now it was taking a new route, going somewhere else, not to the huge pile of waste where he had a claim at the foot of the mountain. It took only a moment. Then the gates opened and closed again, and there was nothing to show that anything out of the ordinary had happened.

King climbed back to the road, so absorbed in what he had seen that he hardly noticed that the snow had virtually ceased.

Ore was being diverted—and while it traveled in the waste chute, he had a hunch that it wasn't dross! Tomorrow would be Sunday. Maybe he could find out where that stuff went!

His thoughts on that possibility, he drove mechanically, taking his place under the chute. Without warning, and before his wagon was fully in place, the gate opened and tons of ore hurtled at him.

King's hat was caught and buried under the ore. He jumped so fast that it came off his head in the path of the dump. The wagon seat splintered and smashed, while stray chunks rattled off the rumps of the wheelers. King landed on his feet on the far side of the wagon, still clutching the reins, holding them steady. The ore continued to cascade until twice a normal load had buried the front end of the wagon and spilled in a small mountain onto the ground on either side.

One horse was kicking, terrified. It was impossible for King to make his voice heard about the noise. Only the impossible weight of the ore kept the teams from running.

From his small hut part way up the hill, where he operated the chute, the whiskery face of the operator popped gopher-like from its window. He craned along neck and peered downward, and it was the speculative light in his eyes, rather than any evidence of shock or horror, which released the fury in King as though another rope had been pulled. Then, his glance ranging past the pile of spilled ore, the operator's glance fixed on Coleman and registered dismay.

A roar erupted from King as he began scrambling up the path alongside the chute, the impetus of anger giving him the appearance of soaring. It was not often that King Coleman lost his temper, but when he did, it was something to see. Now his fury had the quality of an awakened volcano. Three attempts to kill him in about that many days were too many, and all by treachery.

"Come out of there!" he challenged. "Or must I take your cage to pieces and do the same with you! Your hide I will have for the murdering creature you are!"

Had any doubt remained in his mind that the sudden dumping of the ore had been deliberate and not an accident, the look on the operator's face would have dispelled it. There was surprise and consternation, but no show of sorrow or regret. For a moment he hesitated, within the confines of the small hut. Then he came out of it like a cornered woodchuck, taking advantage of his position higher up the hill to come hurtling down.

"If it's trouble you want it's trouble you'll get!" he retorted, and launched himself in a devastating jump, booted feet upraised to crash into King's face and shoulders.

Elevation was furnished by the hill, but his timing was a fraction slow. King ducked flat on the earth, allowing the hobnailed boots and spread-eagled figure to sail above him. From there it was thirty feet to the road, and the operator sailed half the distance before he hit, sliding, a shrill yelp of terror screeching from him. Once down to earth, he kept on until he came to a snow-plowing stop on back and shoulders. He scooted beneath two of the horses and out on the far side.

One of the animals kicked nervously but belatedly. King was reversing his course, but he was forced to circle around the eight horses and back to reach his opponent. By the time he managed it, the other man had regained his feet, only pleasantly stimulated by these preliminaries.

"If it's trouble you want it's trouble you'll get!" he repeated. He had, King decided, a one-track mind. But it was a cold day, and the exercise was warming. King was ready to meet him halfway.

They were behind King's wagon now, in front of the next team, where the road afforded a small open space. At close quarters, as his opponent discovered, King could be rough as a slab of prickly pear. They came together in a smashing impact, and the flurried snow was spattered with blood. It was far from one-sided. King had the fleeting impression that perhaps he'd run up against a kicking mule instead of a man.

All the waiting drivers gathered to watch, but they stood back and made no move to interfere. Flood, masticating a cud of Brown Mule, chewed faster as the chute operator drove a flurry of swinging jabs which staggered King and sent him toward the rail above the gorge. Beyond the rail was the canyon. The other man grinned crookedly past a cut lip, charging with outthrust shoulder to finish it.

King twisted aside and sank reddened knuckles into the bull neck under the hate-bloated face. His fist crunched on the Adam's apple, driving it back into the neck, and his opponent sprawled, gagging sickly. He heaved partially upward with a violent effort, fingers clawing the road. Then he lifted his arm and threw, at point-blank range, a two-pound chunk of the spilled ore straight at King's face.

There was no chance to dodge. King's hand lifted to protect himself. Even then, the missile was too heavy, too fast, completely to control or deflect it. It shagged into his palm with bruising ferocity, gashing along his cheek, shaving skin like an axe blade, tearing loose from his fingers to keep going.

The pain was a needed spur. King had been dazed, uncertain. He roared and leaped, grabbing. His fingers plucked his opponent off the ground and heaved him up like a stuffed doll. Whirling, King released him.

The operator struck on his feet, but they were too tangled to steady him. He staggered backward, hitting the guard rail, and it cracked like the echo of dynamite and broke. For a moment he pawed wildly at air, then started to topple.

King was breathing heavily from his effort. As his

eyes focused, he saw what was happening and jumped.
The other man was on his back, shoulders and arms
over empty air, sliding. King sprawled forward, reaching, grabbing a flailing boot. He clung fast, and Flood
and Moon came to his aid and dragged the man back.

"Whyn't you let him go?" Flood asked disgustedly.
"It's what he was tryin' to do to you."

"It's a long way down," King said soberly. He balled
a handful of snow and wiped blood from his face,
turning to look at the ore which hemmed in the wagon.
Apparently there was no serious damage beyond the
broken seat, but nothing could move until the pile was
cleared.

"Better get shovels and get at it," he suggested.
Then anger burned in his face as Yount came into sight,
hurrying. King confronted him, and now his temper
was icy as the day.

"Did you want some of the same, maybe?" King
demanded, and jerked a contemptuous thumb to where
the operator cowered, the fight gone out of him. "First
you try to kill me in your cage; then you set this hire-
ling to burying me under the ore before I'm even dead!
A quick operation which would take care of both, eh?
A man who fights fair I understand, but such sneaks
as inhabit this hill are beneath the contempt of a fair-
minded coyote!"

Yount's face lost color. He looked about at the scene,

cataloguing what had happened; then his eyes returned to King's.

"I do not blame you for being mad, Coleman," he conceded. "What he did was inexcusable, however he intended it. But I give you my word I had nothing to do with it."

"Nothing, you say? But you are the foreman." Then the anger drained out of King. Somehow he believed the man. "In that case," he sighed, "there is nothing more to be said." And he turned to ride down the mountain.

As though satisfied that it had done enough for one day, the storm was definitely breaking, spots of blue showing through the clouds by the time he reached Charley's Place. There was an appearance of calm in the valley below.

Reaching Silverhill, King stopped his wagon and climbed down to unhook the team. He was driving them toward the barn when Vicki appeared.

She started to speak; then her eyes widened at sight of his face. She came close, reaching to touch his cheek with gentle fingers, and her voice was no more than a whisper.

"What happened, King?"

He explained, making light of it. She would hear in any case. The trouble in her eyes grew deeper.

"This is on account of me," she said, "because you're

trying to help me. It isn't worth it, King. I don't want anything to happen to you."

"It started before you had even asked me," he reminded her. "How is Van Cleeve?"

"There is no change. King, I'm afraid."

"Don't be," he counseled. "We will beat this." But his words carried no assurance. He was about to head for the boarding house when he overheard a couple of miners talking.

"Hard times is right," one growled. "Starving times, if you ask me. But men don't count, of course—only profits!"

"The company got the right man to handle that for them when they hired Apperson," the second growled. "Bloodsucker!"

King turned to the company offices. News of importance was always posted there. Sure enough, there was a poster tacked on one wall of the general room, and men were clustered about it, discussing the matter with a subdued show of anger. King edged close enough to read.

"Notice is hereby given of a curtailment of operations and wages. The company regrets the necessity, but is forced to take action because of economic conditions prevalent throughout the country. To avoid closing down operations completely, economies must be rigidly effected.

"As of Monday, all wages will be lowered by twenty percent. Certain jobs may be suspended indefinitely.

> "By order,
> "B. Apperson, Supt."

10.

The post office at Silverhill was located in a small, partitioned-off room at one end of a general store. Wilma Yount called for the mail, more as a matter of habit than because she expected to receive something of particular interest. Magazines, and a San Francisco weekly newspaper, came upon certain days, and this was not one of them. Aside from those, there was seldom anything worth-while.

It would probably be the same today. A new clerk at the store, assisting with the mail, thumbed through the pile in the general delivery box, then handed her a small bundle. Wilma took it, leafing mechanically through the pile, which were mostly circulars. A small tingle of excitement lightened her eyes, and she half turned back to the clerk, then checked the impulse as she saw that the clerk had already gone to wait on a customer. In the stack was a letter which did not belong in their mail. But there was no real hurry about handing it back.

The error, Wilma reminded herself, was that of the postmaster or the clerk—certainly not her own. Now that she had the letter, it would do no harm to study the outside of it, particularly the return address in the upper corner.

Back at her own house, Wilma did so. The addressee was Miss Vicki Marlow. The return address was Clockman Mines, Boston, Mass.

Wilma's curiosity was whetted. Why should this woman, who was supposedly a newspaper reporter, be receiving mail from such a source? Her eyes narrowed at the singing of the teakettle on the back of the range. It would be a simple matter to steam the envelope open, and later to reseal it. There would be no real harm done, and no one would know the difference—

Having read the letter, she sat awhile, staring at it. Excitement now was like wine in her blood. Here was something of importance. Perhaps she should tell Apperson what she had discovered. It might be vital to him.

On the other hand, this knowledge belonged to her, and it might prove more useful if she kept the secret until some time when it could be turned to real account. Nodding, Wilma resealed the letter and returned it to the post office. Now she had a weapon in the fight which lay ahead.

There was still no change in Van Cleeve's condition the next morning, but the doctor was cautiously optimistic.

"He's alive, and I think he has a fair chance to keep alive," he said. "Nature has its own ways of healing, and this coma is probably good, if it doesn't last too long. We will see."

Vicki's eyes were gravely questioning after the doctor had departed. For the moment, she and King were alone at the bedside.

"I've been thinking about yesterday's accident, King," she said, "and the others which so nearly killed you—that elevator dropping in the mine and all. The men say they think that ore slide yesterday was deliberate."

"I think so, too," he agreed. "It could have been an accident, but the way the operator acted seemed suspicious."

"And this other—when Mr. Van Cleeve's buggy was wrecked. *You* were the man expected along there, weren't you?"

It was no good to make a denial in the face of her deepening concern. King nodded.

"It could have been."

"But why, King? Why are they trying to kill you? Nobody can know what I'm here for—or suspect that you're trying to help me. If I thought that I was leading you into such peril, it wouldn't be worth it."

"They couldn't know," he assured her. "But I've been snooping—I'll be as bad as DeQuille if I keep on! And they're afraid I'm finding out things. They may be right, too," he added. "I'm going to check one angle today, and if it's as I think—you'll have something to report back East."

"I suppose it's useless to ask you not to keep on." She sighed. "You'd do it anyhow, wouldn't you?"

"Once folks start picking on me, I get stubborn," he conceded. "I aim to see this through."

"But I don't want you killed or hurt. Please be careful, King—for my sake!"

"I aim to be." He turned quickly and went from the room, afraid to stay longer, then paused at the door. "Watch out for yourself," he added. "Being a woman wouldn't make much difference, I'm afraid, if they thought you were in the way."

Outside, he encountered Yount, coming toward the boarding house. It was plain that the mine foreman had been seeking him.

"I just wanted a word with you, Coleman," Yount explained. "I told the truth yesterday. I had nothing to do with that ore being spilled on you. On the other hand—" He hesitated uncomfortably. "I guess you've suspected that I sawed that cable of the mine lift. It was a stinkin' thing to do, and I hate myself for it.

But I'd heard that you were an old flame of Wilma's—
and I was crazy jealous—"

He checked, wheezing like a runner, then went on.

"I went crazy, which is no excuse. If you want to
take a swipe at me, I won't hit back."

"It wouldn't be any fun that way," King answered
cheerfully. He eyed the other man almost with com-
passion. I reckon you've had a lot of heartache, eh?"

"You must have known Wilma!" Yount said bitterly.

"We were good friends—a long time ago. There is
nothing between us now, Yount. You can believe that
or not, as you please, but it's so."

"I'm not doubting you—now," Yount returned.
"When I stopped to think, I knew I'd been a fool. This
was going on a long time before you came. But I
wanted you to know."

King went on soberly. He rather liked Yount, even
as he felt sorry for him. It was strange how blind a
man could be at times.

Mindful of how he had been watched before, he
sought out Flood and O'Leary, finding them at the
cabin.

"I'd like a bit of help today," he explained. "I want
to do some exploring—snooping, you might call it. And
it's like enough that there'll be somebody to trail me
and see what I'm about—and, just possibly, to try to
make it hard to come back. It occurred to me that if you

both went ahead of me, but not together, and were where you could do some watching in turn—who knows what you might discover?"

Flood grinned understandingly and reached for his mackinaw.

"And what are we allowed to do if we find a snooper of our own?" he asked.

"It will be a matter for your own judgment. If he allows it, do no more than watch in turn. If you must do more, entreat him tenderly."

"That we will," O'Leary agreed, then shook his head. "If I might make a suggestion, Mike, why don't you trade coats with King? Yours is of an unobtrusive hue, while his is a pattern to knock your eye out. If you could beguile somebody into following *you,* now, then King's work might be less hampered."

Flood was enthusiastic, so King fell in with the idea. They took their departure at separate times. King headed south on the road which led toward the distant smelter, rather than north toward Helltop. The day was clear and sunny and not too cold, and there was a maze of tracks in the snow near the town.

King moved with apparent purpose, cautiously changing course while maintaining a sharp watch. This was a game at which two could play. Flood might already have decoyed DeQuille or whoever was set to watch him, since the mackinaw, if seen from a distance, could easily deceive a watcher. But it was no time to take chances. Three close shaves had been more than enough.

There were tricks which a man learned stalking game, either two or four-legged. By the time he had made a circle, King was satisfied that no one was following him. But he continued to use every ruse at his command.

Working toward a canyon among a maze of hills required hours of hard work. This country was as difficult to traverse as any that he had previously explored, but finally he found what he knew was there. The last quarter-mile was easy, for he came upon wheel tracks, a thin trace along a little used, barely passable route. They led to the other pile of supposed waste. As the crow flies the dump was no more than a quarter of a mile from the other pile, but to reach it involved a roundabout journey of miles.

This pile was of the best grade ore, and enough had collected to fill King's wagons. The trick was to shunt aside an occasional carload, always of the highest grade. When enough was collected here, it could be secretly hauled and sold, and Apperson would pocket the money. Such diversion could account for the difference between a comfortable margin of profit and a net loss for the company.

His mind busy on plans to turn this discovery to

account, King turned back, using as much care in re-tracing his steps as he had in coming, finally emerging below the town. He shucked the coat he'd worn, got back to the cabin and took his ease. Presently Flood showed up.

"I trust you had a good day?" he suggested politely.

"A fine one," King agreed. "And you?"

A beatific grin wreathed Flood's angular features.

"The most fun I've had since we reached these hills," he conceded. "It worked as a man might dream. I dis-covered, as I toiled on my way among the gullies, that someone else was doing the same. So I led him a merry chase, no longer begrudging a skinned shin or the short-ness of breath which I find troubles me at such a task. The poor devil was worn like a misspent dollar bill when I finally came up behind him. He lacked even the energy to jump when I said hello in a friendly fashion."

"DeQuille?"

"DeQuille it was. And the look on his face when he studied the mackinaw and then the face of me, its wearer! I almost felt sympathy for his misspent ener-gies. We passed the time of day, and I headed home-ward; and whether or no he wanders like a lost sheep among the crags, I know not."

King grinned. They would suspect what he had been up to; it would be foolish to underestimate them. A countermove seemed indicated, before they were ready to act. Fortunately, his own wagons were back from the trip to the smelter, ready to be used.

"You have earned your rest, but you're not going to get it," he informed Flood. "Help me round up Moon and the boys, but quietly. Each one that we find will aid in locating the others. We are hitching our teams and going on a jaunt of our own, which may require most of the night. But I think the wages will be worth it."

As it turned out, only nine wagons were available, the tenth being already loaded. They hitched the teams and moved quietly out of town under cover of the night. Being one wagon short, Moon rode with King. He kept silent with some difficulty until they were safely out of town, then exploded.

"Now maybe you'll tell me what this is about," he demanded. "Or am I supposed to choke on my curiosity, like a cow with nails in its cud? After all, I'm a partner in this outfit—or so I assumed."

"You've a right to know," King agreed, "since you're sticking your neck out along with mine. We're going to hijack a few loads of ore—and I think it'll run pretty rich."

"Hijack?" Moon repeated. "The word smacks of piracy. The ethics of such conduct I'll let go for the moment, but how the blazes can the thing be done? For one thing, the chute is empty of ore this night."

"It is empty, and with good reason. Let me fill you in

on some details of my recent activities."

King explained as they went along, while Moon listened in amazement. They swung off from the road, winding about in broken country, while the trail became increasingly difficult.

"And you say this ore has been shunted aside, being especially rich," Moon mused. "In that case, I have but two observations. It is still not ours, and the others, naming no names, will not take kindly to our helping ourselves."

"The money which it brings will go to the owner of the mines, so on that point my conscience is clear," King assured him. "Less, of course, a reasonable wage to us for retrieving and hauling it, which should be a better wage than we have been making; enough, with luck, to show us a bit of profit. As to the other, I have never known you to shun the risk of danger."

"To shun it is one thing," Moon returned glumly. "But we are only ten men—and we'll have a long way to move by the fair light of day. I take it that our route will lead back through the town, along the regular and, as far as I know, the only road to the smelter?"

"In that matter there is no choice."

"Against us Apperson will be able to bring scores of men, should dozens not be sufficient as a deterrent."

"He'll be able to, but he won't," King said confidently. "Much as this will pain him, and he will behave with the proverbial meekness of the lamb."

"If I had not raised you myself, I would think that your brains were addled." Moon sighed. "You tell me just enough to tantalize a man. But I have learned patience to match that of the patriarch Job."

"In that case, take the reins and keep going," King said, and thrust the lines of leather into Moon's hands. "I think I have a chore to attend to."

He was descending when Moon protested.

"So far you have emulated the hog where trouble is concerned," he chided. "Should we not be allowed in on the fun now, whatever it is?"

"I think it will be better if you drive on as though nothing was happening," King returned, and was away from the road at a scrambling run. Moon shook his head in exasperation. He'd seen nothing to cause that hasty departure, but he knew King well enough to be certain that he sought more than exercise.

King had been watching the high hills. There was a moon which wove and dodged between drifting clouds, but since there was snow everywhere, the light was adequate. It was possible that DeQuille had reported his failure of the afternoon, in which case Apperson was likely to jump to conclusions. It was more probable that DeQuille had kept silent as to how he had been fooled, preferring to trust to luck rather than brave the anger of his employer.

But in either case Apperson might take the precaution of having a watchman posted out that way, to make sure that the rich cache of ore was not tampered with. Later, it would be a simple matter to haul it in company wagons, making sure that payment went into a special fund which would reach his own pocket. Judging by the look King had had at the ore, it would run high in silver —well over a hundred dollars to the ton.

King had seen a shadow move on a hilltop a quarter of a mile away. At the same time there had been a glint of light, which might have been the reflection of the moon along a rifle barrel.

Undoubtedly the watchman was alone and would hesitate to challenge ten men. It would be safer and twice as sure to duck back out of sight, climb another hill which towered above all the surrounding peaks, and from that vantage point shoot as a signal. It would be necessary to reach that height; else the ring of hills might smother the sound before it could carry to town or mine.

After it was heard, there would be plenty of time for Apperson to gather a crew and apprehend them in the act of loading the ore, since they lacked a chute and it would have to be shoveled onto the wagons. King preferred to work without interruption.

The watchman was out of sight, but King knew the course he'd follow and took a short cut. The first quarter-mile was easy, but afterward he moved warily. The other man might get nervous if he suspected that he was being followed, and a nervous man could become trigger-happy.

Despite the cold, King was panting with exertion. He saw a line of track too big for anything but a bear or a man, proof that he was not chasing a shadow.

The watcher was getting close to the top where he could fire a signal. King risked a dash across open ground. It was time to move in. He tossed a stone, which fell beside the other man, a litle ahead.

The guard paused, uncertain, not thinking to look elsewhere for danger. By the time he decided to reconnoiter, King was behind him.

"Just drop your gun," King suggested. "You won't be needing it now."

It was disappointingly simple; his own six-gun was a powerful persuader. King picked up the rifle, ejected the shells and handed it back.

"You might as well keep it," he decided. "Let's get back down now."

"What do you think you're going to do?" the watchman challenged as they made their way down to the road, then answered his own question. "Do you think you can get away with stealin' that ore?"

"Why not?" King countered. "Apperson seems to have gotten away with it. I've no doubt he's taken a lot of loads out of here before this. But you don't quite understand. We're not going to steal it."

King had a feeling that the watchman remained unconvinced, but he offered no further protest, even when King suggested that he help shovel the ore onto the wagons. Exercise was necessary to keep warm. Afterward he accepted a ride with them back to town.

All nine wagons were loaded to capacity, and at least they didn't have to make the descent from Helltop. The hours had grown small when they pulled into Silverhill, and no lights shone. The others looked at King expectantly as he gave instructions to unhitch.

"What do we do now?" Moon asked.

"Get some sleep—if we can," King returned. "It'll be little enough."

"So it will. But do we leave these wagons here in plain sight?"

"Where else? We aren't stealin' the stuff," King repeated. "And we couldn't hope to reach the smelter before being overtaken."

"That," Moon sighed, "is the way I figure it."

11.

King was one of the first astir in the camp, and darkness still blanketed the valley when he and Moon emerged from breakfast and harnessed their teams. The other boarders had eaten almost in silence, an indication that word of the hijacking was not yet public.

King was disappointed that Vicki did not show up. He'd hoped to see her before starting the trip to the smelter. Van Cleeve, when he looked in on him, still slept as though he might never awaken.

Gray slabs were prying loose the gloom as they hitched their teams to the wagons.

Voices and the clomp of booted feet along icy sidewalks broke the silence, and from the sound, many men were coming. They hove in sight, Apperson at their head—a full score, armed as for a hunting expedition. The watchman was with them, and he grinned cheerfully. Moon surveyed them gloomily.

"I doubt that they are a committee of well-wishers, come to speed us on our way," he opined dourly.

Apperson wasted no time with preliminaries. His

tone held as angry rasp.

"Ah! What do you think you're about, Coleman—stealing?"

King looked at him with shocked surprise.

"Stealing?" he repeated. "Now where would you learn such a naughty word, Apperson? It's one I'd not have expected to fall from your lips."

Apperson's face reddened. He set foot on a wheel hub and climbed to peer over the side.

"Then what would you call it?" he asked with elaborate sarcasm. "Do you know a better word?"

"Why, I'd call it hauling," King replied. "That's what we're here for—to haul the ore out and take it to the smelter. A man needs a change of scenery now and then, so we'll take the low road a spell, instead of the hilltop."

"The low road is a good description," Apperson agreed, still sarcastic. "As for a change of scenery, perhaps you'll like the view better from the penitentiary."

"That I would doubt. But you may know whereof you speak—in regard to the pen."

Apperson's face had a bloated look.

"You bet I know what I'm taking about," he growled. "Stealing is a mighty serious business—enough to send all of you up for long terms!"

"Why now, maybe you've investigated the matter," King conceded. "I would, if I wore your boots. But be

careful how you bandy words. I'm a patient man, but
there are limits. You know, of course, having snoopers
as you do, that I've filed on a claim of land, called a
homestead, where the waste from the mine is dumped.
Also, I'm sure you'll have been informed that I made
doubly certain by staking a mineral claim."

"I know about that," Apperson snapped. "Are you
claiming that this ore came from the dump?"

"Where else?" King asked innocently. He shook his
head, looking about at Moon and the others. "Where
on earth else should it come from? Where else *could*
it? Could you tell me that now, man?"

Flood chuckled. Apperson was suddenly speechless,
pondering the question. As he considered the implica-
tions, his face took on the look of the snow, purpled
like a turkey gobbler's, then paled again as his anger
seemed to be doing. He stared in bafflement.

Flood broke into a roar of laughter, and the rest of
the crew, including Moon, joined as they understood the
hoax. Apperson was stymied. He dared not admit that
the ore had come from a separate dump where it had
been shuttled by his orders. To concede that would be
to admit himself a thief. And King had nine witnesses
whose testimony could send him to that pen of which
he had been talking so glibly.

King spat casually on Apperson's boot and gathered
up the reins.

"Since you discarded it, it belongs to the land where it rests," he pointed out. "Maybe there's not so much waste in this as you supposed. Anyhow, we're hauling these loads to the smelter to find out." He clucked to his horses.

Apperson stared, baffled and enraged. He contented himself with a weak threat.

"If you go off that way without permission, you're fired!" he howled.

King chuckled.

By comparison with the descent from Helltop, the journey to the smelter was in the nature of a vacation. There were stretches of bad road, ice and snow, but the journey was made without incident. As King anticipated, he had no difficulty selling the ore. The smelter was independent, and Apperson, after painful second thoughts, had raised no protests.

The price was as good as King had hoped for—over six thousand dollars for the nine loads. That proved his suspicion, that only unusually rich cars of ore were shunted aside in such fashion. Probably no more would be given that treatment, at least until he had been disposed of.

He had no doubt that this was a temporary lull.

Back in town, the weather had turned warm and pleasant. The snow on the hills was untouched, but there was mud and slush in the streets; weather to make a man feel good. There were other things to make him happy—the prospect of a good supper, and of seeing Vicki again. The days away had taught him that she mattered more than anything else.

Having left the teams at the barn, he was halfway to the boarding house when he encountered Apperson. The foreman stopped, apparently surprised at seeing him.

"So you're back!" Apperson said angrily. "You're wasting your time!"

"Now that," King returned, "is a matter for argument, but I don't feel in the mood just now. It has been too pleasant a day to spoil."

"Then, if your waste from the dump is so valuable, you can go right on hauling it," Apperson suggested bitingly. "There's no work for any of you with the mines."

King waved that aside airily. Vicki was coming from the kitchen, a bowl in her hands, as he entered. Her face took on a warmer hue, perhaps the effect of the big range above which she had been bending.

"King! You're back!" she said.

"I'm back," he agreed, "and glad to be. There are magnets and there are lodestones, but none have half the power to attract of that which lures me home again!"

She colored more richly, but was not to be diverted from an anxious concern.

"You had a good trip?"

"The best. Can you spare a moment for a word by ourselves?" He winked at Moon, about to take his place at table, and smiled at DeQuille, who scowled. "I think you will find my news interesting," he added.

Vicki nodded and led the way to the seldom used parlor. King closed the door.

"How is Van Cleeve?" he asked.

"Better. He's been conscious the past two days, and the doctor thinks he'll be all right."

"That is good news, but I have better. It concerns the ore we hauled. For it I was paid some six thousand dollars." From his pocket he produced a large sheaf of bills and began to thumb them through. "Money, legal tender. It belongs to the company, therefore to the young lad whose interests you so graciously represent—"

"But I—how can it be company money?" she stammered. "If it was from ore you hauled from the waste—"

"Ore it was, and where I hauled it from Apperson understood," King explained. "It was diverted from the regular chute. So if you will send the cash East, minus a ten percent fee for hauling, which under the circumstance seems a fair price—"

"Of course it's fair," she agreed. "To the company, that is; maybe not to you. But what is this I hear about you being fired?"

"All too true, I expect. It seems that Apperson is somewhat annoyed with me. The matter will require some adjustment."

"But you can't be fired — it wouldn't do." Vicki frowned at him, pulling at her lower lip in sudden preoccupation. "You've got to have a job, and it has to be with the company, so that you can stay on here—"

"The temptation is almost more than a man can bear—even such a man as myself. Those lips, when you pucker them in that fashion—" King leaned suddenly and kissed her. Vicki's cheeks colored, but she did not draw away. After a moment, her arms crept up about his neck.

"Now this is a homecoming to remember," King said finally, looking into her eyes. "It is what I've dreamed of all those days on the road. It—"

Vicki interrupted. Her voice was demure, but her eyes sparkled.

"You kiss quite satisfactorily, sir," she informed him, then checked him with an uplifted palm. "But am I to assume, from your conduct, that it is your intention to marry me?"

"I could not have put it better myself." King grinned. "At the moment, I can think of no higher ambition, or one with which I could more heartily concur."

"Since the gentleman proposes, the lady is pleased to accept his kind offer," Vicki murmured, then danced away as he sought to catch her again. "Wait. There is business to discuss, and the supper will grow cold."

"Food," King said grandly, "is for the soul. Man does not live by bread alone."

"But this is important. Apperson has really fired you?"

"Such seemed to be the import of his words."

"Then," Vicki said decisively, "he'll just have to hire you again." She turned to the big desk at the corner, seated herself and drew a tablet toward her. Uncorking a bottle of ink, she dipped the pen, then frowned in thought. After a moment she wrote rapidly. Then, blotting the sheet, she handed it to him.

"Give this to Mr. Apperson in the morning," she instructed.

King read it, then read again, more slowly, frowning. The missive was direct.

"To Mr. Bart Apperson, acting foreman for The Clockman Mines. You will employ Mr. Coleman, his crew, wagons and teams, at a price mutually satisfactory."

It was signed, "M. M. Clockman."

King raised his eyes. "I don't understand," he said.

Vicki's were still dancing, "It's simple," she explained. "My name is Michael Marlow Clockman—the Michael for Mike, since my dad wanted a boy and sort of had to compromise. Michael was shortened to Mickey; then somebody twisted it to Vicki, while I was still very young. The Vicki has stuck. So when I decided to come out here and do some snooping on my own account, it seemed a wise precaution to come as Vicki Marlow, which is my name. But Apperson has never heard of anyone except M. M. Clockman."

King stood assimilating the news. It was rather a big dose for one quick swallow.

"So you're the owner of Clockman Mines," he said finally. "The heiress to all this bonanza of wealth—"

"Which has turned out to be *borrasco* instead of bonanza, so far," she said quickly. "This—" she fingered the roll of bills he had tendered— "is the first real dividend since my father died."

"I'm glad of the dividend," King said soberly. "But stealing or poor management, or both, doesn't stop it from being a bonanza. You should be a very rich young lady, Miss Clockman—"

"To you it is Vicki," she informed him serenely. "Why do you think I almost threw myself at your head just now, in a manner scarcely ladylike? One reason was that I was afraid you'd climb on your high horse if you found out who I was. But you're too late, my man. You've proposed marriage, and I've accepted. And I warn you, I have no intention of allowing you to back out of your obligations. Besides, King," she added, and ducked under an arm to nestle close to him, "I love you.

Also, I need you very much. Without you to see to these mines and handle Bart Apperson, I'll be no heiress, but a pauper."

King recognized the undeniable truth of what she said and surrendered.

"Sure, and I couldn't resist you, sweetheart, with or without such an appeal," he admitted. "Somehow it seems that I've fallen in love with you."

"It happened to me when you first swooped me into your arms," she admitted unblushingly. "But now the supper will be getting cold."

"Let it!"

"And everybody will be wondering—and raising their eyebrows—and talking—"

"We'll explain—"

"But do we want to—and have it known who I am? The way I worded that order, it can seem as though you have had it in your possession all along, holding it for use only if required. Of course, if you want to go and fire Mr. Apperson, that's all right with me—"

King nodded slowly.

"Perhaps we had better dine," he decided. "It would be a pleasure to fire Apperson, but for the moment it may be expedient to give him a bit more rope. I don't know that he's quite yet ready to hang himself."

"But we can tell Ma Travis and the boarders that we are going to be married," Vicki said. "They'll be sure to notice how my hair is mussed—I must look a sight—"

"You're a sight for sore eyes," King assured her. "And I see through your ruse. But don't worry. I'll even take the mines along with you, since you seem to have inherited 'em." He eyed her more closely. "That makes you the daughter of old Zeb, doesn't it?"

"I guess it does," she agreed. "I never knew my father very well—which I've regretted as I grew older. Poor old Dad! He couldn't stand any life except the one he lived, and Mother couldn't stand that. I think I'd have liked it. So she and I lived most of the time back East, and he kept on alone, hoping to make his strike. Mother was able to help him after he made it, because she knew people who had money." She was silent a moment. "But we had better not mention who I am."

"Just who you're going to be," King agreed, and grinned at the others as they returned to the dining room. "We've been discussin' somethin' important," he confided. "This little lady's done me the honor of agreein' to marry me. Which makes me the luckiest man in the state of Nevada, not to mention California—and a few others that could just as well be tossed in for good measure."

There was a chorus of exclamations and congratulations. DeQuille did not join in them. After a moment he arose and slipped out of the room.

12.

Yount ate his supper in a brooding silence. Wilma watched him anxiously, fighting a growing apprehension which she could not down. She had become accustomed to his occasional rages, to a driving impatience which had been matched by her own. She had whetted that impatience, trying to spur him on to better jobs, to greater accomplishment. Only of late had she grown disillusioned, accepting the fact that he had probably gone as far as he was capable of going. You couldn't, she reflected bitterly, make an executive out of a mucker.

For the past several days there had been no show of rage on his part, no further bursts of impatience, no jealous reproofs or upbraiding. Instead, Yount went about his tasks like a man asleep. It frightened her. Until Apperson's plan reached its culmination and a change could be made, she had to remain penned up there with Yount. Penned was the word. There was no escape until Apperson was ready to take her away.

Watching, her qualms sharpened. Maybe she had

gone too far, driven Yount too hard. Certainly she didn't want any change until the time was ripe for it.

Today she had gone to considerable trouble to prepare an appetizing supper, to make things as comfortable and pleasant as possible for Yount. But he had not seemed to notice.

He scraped back his chair, moved wearily to the hooks on the wall and lifted down his heavy coat and cap. Then he turned.

You'd better start packin'," he said heavily.

"Packing?" Terror put a quaver into her voice. Was he kicking her out—instead of it being the other way around, as she had so often envisioned? "What do you mean?"

"What I say." He looked at her, his eyes dark, somber. "You've always hated this camp. You've told me that a hundred times. Well, you won't have to stick around much longer. We're getting out. Pack what there is."

"But I don't understand." She leaned against the wall, suddenly feeling that her limbs might give way. It wouldn't do to leave now. She knew with a dismal certainty that if she went elsewhere to wait for Apperson, it would be a long wait indeed. As long as she was there, he found her a pleasant companion. But if she were out of sight, she would soon be out of mind as well.

"This is your job," she went on quickly, "the best job

you've ever had. You can't—"

"I'm quitting!" The words came harshly, as though torn from somewhere deep inside him. "This has been a bad town for us. We're leaving."

"Are your crazy," Wilma demanded wildly, "to throw up a good job, with times as hard as they are? We'll starve—"

Something in his look stopped her. His voice dripped with bitterness.

"*You* wouldn't starve!" he said. "You'll always contrive to find something—somebody—to batten on!" Cold raced across the room at the opening of the door. It seemed to remain after the door closed.

Winter had shown what it could do when it took a notion. Now, as though relenting, the weather had turned pleasant. The air was almost balmy the next morning, as King and the others threw harnesses on the big horses and then hooked the teams together, afterward driving them to the wagons and hitching them in place.

They had used their own wagons for the journey to the smelter, so today again they would have them for the trip to the hilltop.

King had stopped twice to see Van Cleeve—evening and morning. Each time, however, the assayer had been asleep, and King had not wanted to waken him.

Moon approached King, an edge of doubt in his voice.

"We're hitchin' up," he pointed out. "But where are we going? You got somethin' in mind?"

"Why, to work," King returned absently. His thoughts had moved in easy sequence from the sick man to Vicki, who had been watching over him. Vicki had been increasingly in his mind for the past few weeks, and after last evening, day dreaming had become as pleasant as the best night dreams had ever been.

"Work, eh?" Moon was elaborately casual. "Being fired from a job makes no never-mind, eh?"

King grinned at him. "Not a bit," he conceded. "We'll stop at the company offices as we go past. Since you're in on this, you might as well come into the office and see the fun, if you like."

"I'll sure go along," Moon agreed. "But as to fun— I'll wait and see."

As it happened, it was not necessary to go inside the building. Daylight was brushing away the patches of darkness like a sweeping broom, and Apperson, noticing the approach of the wagons, came out to stop them. His mood was truculent.

"Ah! And where do you think you're going?" he demanded. "This road, in case you don't know, leads to Helltop."

"And well-named it is," King agreed affably. "Would

you be intimatin' that there is no ore ready for the hauling?"

"There's none for you to haul. I told you before that you're fired. How many times do I have to repeat it? You're through—washed up, finished."

"The man has a glib tongue for adjectives," King said admiringly. "But take a look at this now, Mister Foreman." He leaned down to extend the order which Vicki had written the evening before. "You'll observe that it's an order from the boss—and I mean the boss —to employ us. Which, of course, is a favor to you, since you have need of our services."

Apperson stared incredulously at the order. He had seen that signature too many times to doubt its authenticity, and now his worst fears were confirmed. Coleman wasn't doing all this on his own. He was there as a representative of Clockman, and if there had been the smell of disaster before, now it loomed like a tangible presence.

Mike Flood spoke from where he watched, a ribald quality to his tone.

"The man doesn't look as though he knew a favor when he gets slapped in the face with one, King!"

King clucked to his team. "We are sometimes slow to appreciate our blessings." He sighed. "Nonetheless, they come."

He drove on, the others following. Apperson watched

them go. Once or twice he opened his mouth, but no words came.

Presently the wagons were out of sight, beginning the long climb. In certain respects it was an unusual road, those twisting miles to the top of the mountain. Now and again it leveled off, but not once was there a dip on the way up. All the steepness was reserved for the down-grade, when the wagons descended under a heavy burden.

Some of that burden seemed to have settled on Apperson's shoulders as he retreated slowly to the sanctuary of his office. He had the queasy sensation he was being played with, like a mouse making sport for a cat before it became a meal.

He was still superintendent of the Clockman Mines, as far as the title went. Coleman hadn't bothered to fire him, but there was no longer any doubt in Apperson's mind that King had the authority to do so when and if he chose, and that he certainly intended to do so before long.

Coleman had come to camp in an ambiguous role, getting a job, talking to people, looking around, ferreting out secrets which Apperson had been sure were well hidden. And now—

Now he was still waiting. For what? Coleman knew that Apperson had been mulcting the company. Perhaps he'd grown overbold with success, careless because of his belief that Clockman was a fool who could be satisfied with explanations and an occasional check, who considered himself too good to soil his boots in so crude an atmosphere.

But he had been shrewd enough to send a representative who'd wormed his way in clever fashion. Coleman now had evidence enough to warrant discharging Apperson. Since he hadn't done so, but was making a pretense of going on as before, in the same old job, it could mean only one thing. He and Clockman would not be satisfied merely with firing Bart. They intended to send him to the penitentiary.

The delay could only mean that Coleman wasn't too sure as yet of his evidence. He was waiting to get an iron-clad case, proof which would stand up in court.

Apperson smiled sourly. Coleman would have a long wait. He had played it pretty cagily, and this delay was in the nature of a reprieve. He'd make use of it—

Apperson started, scowling, at a rap on the door. He didn't want to see anybody at the moment. He needed time to think, to devise a counter-plan, one which this time must be fool-proof. He could not afford any more bungling.

He arose impatiently, strode to the door and flung it open. His harsh question died unspoken. Wilma stood there, apprehension in her eyes. Apperson stepped back to allow her to enter, but he was frowning anew.

"What the devil are you doing here, Wilma?" he demanded roughly. "You should know better than to come to my office in broad daylight—"

"As the wife of your mine foreman, I might have business here," Wilma retorted. "But I had to come, Bart. It's important. There's trouble—big trouble."

Apperson sank back in his chair while she took another. He could see that she had been crying.

"You're telling me!" he growled. "What's wrong? Has Yount been beating you?"

"No. But he says he's quitting—that we're leaving here—"

"If it rains cats, you can be mighty sure there'll be dogs to chase 'em." Apperson grimaced. This was news to him. Yount hadn't bothered to tell him of his intention of resigning and that wasn't good. He needed Yount now, in the mounting crisis.

And in case Yount didn't care to go along with his plans—well, Yount wouldn't have much choice. Bart knew too much of his foreman's recent activities for Yount to refuse.

"What the devil is he quitting for?" Apperson demanded. "He doesn't know—"

"About us?" Wilma finished. "I don't know. I don't suppose so. If he did—" She shivered. "He's acting very strangely. He doesn't talk or get mad—just looks at me. Last evening he said we'd made a mistake coming here, that he was quitting and we were leaving. I thought you'd know."

"It's news to me," Apperson confessed. "Rats desert a sinking ship!" he added bitterly. "He must have gotten scared."

"Nothing ever scares him," Wilma returned. It was true. Whatever qualities Yount might or might not have, nothing ever scared him. "What are we going to do?" she added.

"That's what I'm trying to figure out," Apperson confessed. "Look at this." He thrust the order across at her. "Where do you think I got it?"

Wilma read it, frowning, and was quick to understand.

"Coleman?"

"Who else? He gave it to me just a few minutes ago, when I told him again that he was fired. You can see what this means. He's here to snoop for Clockman—and he's found out plenty!"

Wilma couldn't resist a taunt. "Haven't you covered your trail?" she demanded.

"There'd have been no trouble, except that he found that cache of ore. I thought the way of handling that was fool-proof. There've been other snoopers before," he added. "But they never discovered anything."

That was not strictly accurate. A couple of men, whom he suspected of having been sent out by his employer, had found out things. But they had not lived to report their findings.

"And you thought you knew how to handle him," Wilma agreed. She was thinking hard, striving to evaluate the situation. She had been right about King—he was a far better man than any she'd ever had anything to do with. If only he had been willing to take up again where they had left off so long before—

But there was no profit in such speculation. He'd made it abundantly clear how he felt about her, and this morning the news of his engagement to that other girl was all over town. It had been the shock of that report, on top of the rest, which had sent her hurrying to see Apperson.

"I wish I knew exactly how much authority he has," Apperson went on. "Maybe he figures that he has to communicate with Clockman before he can take any further action. It all depends on how much authority he was given. That would give me a couple of weeks, before he could send a letter and get a reply back. If I only had some way of knowing—"

"You have," Wilma said. This was going to give him a jolt, and he wouldn't like it, but it was valuable information, which he needed. Also, it would place him in her debt. "The answer's right here in town."

"What do you mean?" Apperson stared at her. "I'm talking about Clockman—"

"So am I. That was what I really wanted to see you about. I've found out that the big boss—M. M. Clockman—is here in town—now!"

Apperson stared, losing color, breathing hard. "How do you know?" he gasped, and looked hastily about, as though expecting to see some dread figure suddenly materialize from the shadows.

"She's been here for a couple of weeks," Wilma informed him calmly. "I had a lucky break yesterday—"

"She? What the devil are you talking about?"

"Wait a minute, and I'll tell you. The postmaster made an error yesterday, and I found a letter in my mail which didn't belong there." It would be safer to mention the day before than to let him know that she had held such information secret until a time when it might come in handy.

"The letter was addressed to Miss Vicki Marlow—but it had a return address on the envelope: The Clockman Mines, Boston."

Apperson blinked, trying to grasp the significance of that.

"You mean—?"

"I mean that I got to thinking, and since the letter had been handed to me, I decided that it might be a good idea to steam it open before I returned it to the post office. So I did. There was plenty in it. Vicki Marlow is M. M. Clockman. One of the M's in her name is for Marlow—her mother's name, I take it."

There was silence while Apperson considered that. He had no reason to doubt the accuracy of what she had told him, for it fitted only too well. He, too, had heard the report that the girl and King Coleman were planning to be married. Trouble had begun with their arrival—together. Yes, it fitted very well.

"I never had any notion that old Zeb's heir was a girl," he mused. "If I'd known that—"

"If you'd known that, and how young and pretty she was, you'd have handled matters differently and done your best to marry her," Wilma finished. "But you didn't know—and it's too late now to get any notions along those lines."

That was only too true. The thing he had feared most had happened. The boss was there in town, and had been there long enough to find out what was going on. Of course she had written that order for Coleman either last evening or this morning. He could be fired at any time—

But so far it hadn't suited their purpose to do so. Coleman was waiting—but this information gave Apperson leverage. He knew who Vicki Marlow was, and they didn't suspect that he knew. Apperson blinked at the ceiling, and Wilma, aware that he was thinking hard, did not interrupt.

Slowly his tense face relaxed, and she knew that he

was getting an idea. He glanced at her speculatively, then leaned forward across the desk.

"I think I've got it, Wilma," he said. "What you've told me makes all the difference. But I'll need your help."

"What do you want?"

"You don't like this Vicki, do you?"

Wilma saw no reason to conceal her spite. "I'd like to claw her eyes out!"

"Naturally. But you've had no trouble with her, I hope?"

"There's been no occasion for any."

"What I want, then," he said, "is for you to take a buggy and team of horses and go for a drive. Hunt her up, and suggest brightly that you're going for a ride to the top of the hill. You understand that she's interested in getting pictures of the mines, and you'd like company. You're two women together, almost the only two who might be congenial in such a place, so you thought of her. You know."

"Why do you want me take her up on a high mountain?" Wilma demanded suspiciously. "Am I supposed to push her off after I get her up there?"

"It would be all right with me. But what I have in mind is to give her the royal treatment. Stop at Charley's on the way up for coffee and pie. That will give me time to get to the top ahead of you. Besides, you'll need to wait at the halfway point for the wagons to come down, before you go on up."

"But what's going to happen at the top?"

"We'll show her the kingdoms of this world—the mines—you and I together. If we can lull her suspicions, get a few days in which to work—then I have a plan. Now this is important. We can't let her suspect that we guess who she is. But if you take her for a ride, and I happen to be there and, as superintendent, offer to show you both around, because I've heard that she's representing an Eastern paper—do you begin to get the idea?"

"I guess so," Wilma conceded. "Maybe it will help."

"It's got to," Apperson said sharply. "I'll get the rest of it worked out and tell you afterward. We're playing for high stakes—and believe me, I know what I'm doing!"

13.

Once engaged upon the project, Wilma threw herself into it with enthusiasm. It was a pleasant day for a ride, and though thought of the road up the mountain made her shiver, she assured herself that it was safe enough. As long as the big ore wagons could make the journey, a light buggy should have no trouble. A team could hold to the trail with ease.

When the horses were tied outside, she presented herself at the boarding house and sought out Vicki, extending her hand smilingly.

"I'm Wilma Yount, and I've been wanting to meet you," she said. "I'm going up on the hill, and I wondered if you wouldn't like to ride along. You can get a good look at the mines and take some pictures, and it will give us a good chance to get acquainted, though I already feel as if we were old friends."

She enlarged upon that theme, once Vicki had accepted and they were leaving the town behind.

"King has told me about you," Wilma said unblushingly. "I used to know him, years ago. Then, when I heard the news today—and of course it's all over town —that he and you were going to be married, I decided I couldn't wait any longer to meet you. One of these days, we'll have to arrange a party for you folks by way of celebration."

She was not sure how well the line was going over. Vicki was friendly, but for the most part she listened rather than divulged confidences. *She's a shrewd piece,* Wilma decided, and thought enviously: "She's getting everything I ever wanted—a fortune, and King!" But she allowed none of her jealousy to show in her face or voice. Between them, she and Apperson must somehow persuade this girl that everything was going well, that Apperson was working hard for her interests. That was of primary importance.

The sun shone brightly, was almost too sharp for comfort on the endless white of the big hill. The air was exhilarating. Two or three times they encountered lines of men, miners, descending toward the camp. They lifted hands in polite gesture to caps and took the outside of the road, allowing the buggy to hug the cliff. Sometimes there was scant room to spare, with the slopes at the side breath-taking.

The effect of the sun and the wagons was to coat the road with ice. This was somewhat roughened by shod hoofs; nonetheless it could be very slick. There was rarely enough heat to melt it away.

"This makes me hungry," Wilma declared as they reached the halfway point. "We'll have a cup of coffee and something to eat at Charley's. Besides, we'll have to wait for the wagons that will soon be coming down.

"I was certainly surprised," she went on, leading the way inside. "Charley makes the best pie! Somehow it seems strange that a Chinaman should be able to make good pie."

Charley himself served them, smiling blandly. The quality of the food was up to standard. They waited while the ore wagons passed—six of them—then were given word that the others had been delayed and would wait until they had reached the top. There were always signals and instructions when extra vehicles made the trip.

They returned to the buggy, Wilma untying the hitch rein. Everything was going nicely. She climbed to the seat, taking up the reins. The road narrowed sharply beyond the wide spot, climbing steeply. At the side was the first real drop-off—a cliff falling sheer away for hundreds of feet.

Wilma clucked to the horses, then started involuntarily. Yount was approaching, a look of surprise on his face at sight of them. With an effort, Wilma forced a smile to her own.

"Hello, honey," she called. "I didn't expect to see you until we got on up. Vicki, I want you to meet my husband."

Yount nodded shortly, ungraciously. The suspicion which Wilma had seen so many times of late was sharp on his face.

"What are you going up the hill for today?" he demanded. "And whose idea was it?"

Wilma tried to laugh lightly, and found the sound clogging like freezing ice in her throat.

"Why, it was my idea," she said. "It was such a nice day and everything—"

"Wait a minute." It was a command, not a suggestion. Scowling, Yount moved around the buggy. He reached and fumbled at the hub of the right rear wheel —the wheel which traveled at the outer edge of the road as they climbed.

"Whose idea was it?" he repeated harshly, and with a single twist of thumb and finger, removed the nut and held it up for them to see. Wilma's eyes widened, but Yount went on implacably.

"I just noticed somebody skulking away from the buggy, acting like he was up to something. This would have dropped off just about as you started to climb— and so would the wheel." He gestured toward the abyss below, and needed no words to tell what would have happened on that stretch of ice. *"Whose idea was it for you to come up here?"*

Wilma's blood was like ice; the cold coursed all through her body. Abruptly it was all clear. Apperson was making use of the information she had given him, but he was making use of her as well. She was the perfect tool for his purpose, and if he had felt any qualms at offering her as a sacrifice, those had been outweighed by his need. With him, it was always himself first.

If Vicki, who owned the mines, should meet with a fatal accident, which would be attributed to Wilma's foolishness—then there would be no one with the authority to fire him or to prosecute! King Coleman would still have to be reckoned with, but Apperson would be planning to handle him as well. This had become a matter of self-preservation, and to attain that Apperson would stop at nothing.

"It was Apperson's idea," Wilma answered, "even to the time, so that we'd have to stop here for something to eat while the wagons passed—and to give somebody a chance to loosen that nut, I suppose!"

Yount's face did not change. It was as though he were beyond hurt or surprise. Wordlessly he tightened the nut again, made a quick check of the other wheels, and motioned with his arm for them to turn around and get back to town. Wilma was only too glad to obey. Her hands were shaking so that she could scarcely hold the reins. After a moment, Vicki reached over and took them.

Moon came plodding back as the wagons stood in line at the turn, waiting their chance to load from the chute. There was a new man working the chute today, and King noticed that he was careful to have each wagon precisely in place before he loosed any ore. King's wagon was behind Moon's.

"I've been thinkin'," Moon said without preamble. "Call it a hunch. I want to trade wagons, King."

"Trade?" King repeated. "Why? Don't tell me yours jounces or something?"

"It settles your breakfast, all right," Moon agreed. "But it's this way, King. It's you that've been stirrin' up grudges, and somebody has tried to get you sev'ral times already. I got a notion mebby they'll be tryin' again, and where'd be a better time or a worse place than on the way down today? So if I was to ride your wagon, we might sort of fool 'em some."

King's face softened to a smile, even as he shook his head.

"You mean fool yourself?" he asked. "Where'd be the gain if they picked on you?"

"It ain't me they're after, so that wouldn't necessarily follow. Lookin' twice, anybody'd recognize me, then call off their dogs. But in that much time, 'fore they located you—even a mite of delay around one of these curves could spoil a plan. Think of it from Vicki's standpoint, King. You've won yourself a mighty fine girl, and a sweet one. So you can't go on being bull-headed and selfish and thinkin' only of yourself. You got to start thinkin' of her, too. If anything was to happen to you, where'd she be?"

King had been thinking of that. Vicki was Zeb Clockman's daughter, and at this juncture she needed him. Moon saw the indecision in his face and pressed the point.

"It ain't likely to make a bit of difference to me, one way or another, but it might make some to you, in case anybody was schemin'," he urged. "Just the fact of you being a different place in the line could save you. So climb down now."

King shrugged and complied.

"Since you put it that way, I'll do it," he agreed. "Though if something should happen to you—"

"Oh, nothin's going to bother me. My luck's runnin' high, wide an' handsome these days. Not to suggest that Maggie's wide-built, which she ain't, but you get what I mean."

King went on to the next wagon, climbed to the seat and gathered up the reins. There were wagons ahead and behind. The noise of ore, sliding along the chutes, sounded intermittently. King found himself

listening to the growl of the waste. Today there was
no change which would indicate that some was being
shuttled off to the secret chute. It was unlikely if that
would be used again.

He got his load, then went on as Moon pulled up
behind. There was perhaps a quarter of a mile of easy
descent where the horses had no difficulty holding the
load, merely by planting their calked hoofs firmly and
easing back in the harness. After that the first steep
pitch was ahead.

Moon was not far behind, and the others were strung
out behind him. The wagons ahead were out of sight.
Today there were no clouds, and a breathless hush
seemed to grip the mountain, broken only by the slide
or squeal of wheels on the ice. Silverhill, glimpsed from
the turn, showed like a smudge against the otherwise
spotless earth.

The horses plodded around the bend, and the town
was shut away. King reached for the brake, shoving it
forward with his foot, keeping his boot on the bar
to exert a steady pressure. The wheels squealed as pressure came, and the wagon slewed as they locked and
slid. The horses, trained for such emergencies, did not
change the even tempo of their descent, and the slide
was quickly checked.

King looked back. Moon's horses were just coming
into sight around the curve. Even as his head turned,

there was a sharp crack, like the pop of a pistol.

Moon's face lost its ruddiness. He called urgently to his team, straining back on the reins, seeking with the force of his own will to hold them steady. His voice remained soothing and calm, with a reassuring quality.

There was need of reassurance. The teams were doing their best, striving to hold back on the slick steepness of the road, but they were being pushed, shoved to a quick walk which broke into a ragged trot. King needed no blueprint of what had happened. When Moon had started to brake, the rod had snapped.

How or why it had broken was not a matter of immediate consequence. It had given way, and now Moon was without a brake on a heavily loaded wagon. The entire strain was upon the horses.

On a dry road, they might be able to hold even such a burden. But on glare ice, with the wheels sliding as though on grease, the wagon was fast assuming control. The trot was changing to a run; their holding power was all but gone.

Not far below was another turn, and below that many more. The next one was what counted. They'd reach it at too great a speed to make the turn; even if the horses got around the curve, the hurtling weight of the wagon would whip outward and off, jerking them like the tail to a kite.

Moon was shouting above the hard clatter of hoofs

and grind of wheels.

"Hug the bank! Get in close!"

King knew what Moon planned to do. He figured on staying with the wagon, jerking the reins to swing the teams outward so that they'd miss King's wagon and spill off without compounding the disaster.

Had the road been clear, except for Moon, he might have jumped and saved himself, but to do so now would leave time for his panic-stricken team to hurtle into King's outfit and carry it with them. Moon's hunch regarding trouble had been correct. Now he was prepared to sacrifice himself to save King.

King had a different idea. There wasn't much time or space in which to maneuver, but there was a chance. The road was fairly wide along there—narrow for two vehicles to pass, though on a dry road it could be done, if the driver who took the outer rim had steady nerves.

King shoved harder on the brake, speaking to his own horses, lifting an arm in an imperative gesture to Moon. At the same time he swung his horses, not toward the bank, but outward.

Moon saw what King intended, and groaned. But he knew instantly that he had to follow King's lead. There was no longer a chance to swing his outfit to the brink and send it off. Such a move would mean disaster for both. King's outward move, coupled with the shortening space between and the hurtling speed of Moon's descent, left no time.

Moon's weight was on the threads of leather; his feet were braced. He still maintained a semblance of control, but he had the sensation of trying to lift himself by his bootstraps. It was up to King now—to King and his team, though Moon would help as best he could.

It was going to be a close thing, one way or the other. The curve was just ahead, and they had to stop short of it or go to destruction together, sixteen horses, two wagons and two men locked in a hopeless tangle.

It was a game which had to be played out to the last possible second, for victory was impossible short of that. That would leave no time to jump if the gamble failed.

King's wagon was at the outer edge, leaving a space between it and the high bank. Moon nosed his leaders in, and it was crowded worse than three in a love seat. King's wagon had slowed to a crawl; the brake and horses were in full control. But the big outer wheels were cracking the crust of ice along the brink, sending flakes spilling over.

There was the additional hazard that King's horses might panic as the others came thundering up, crowding between them and the safety of the bank, spurred by panic. King was fighting that terror with voice and hand, looking back, gauging the distance as the second wagon came plowing into the opening. The bend of the road was just ahead.

And around it now, plodding toward their work, came a score of the miners!

The men were taken by surprise, the bend of the hill having blanked out sound as well as sight. And there was no room for them on the road—not with two teams and wagons abreast.

King saw, and swung his leaders toward the bank, crowding hard against Moon's teams, increasing the risk of panic. If the teams, close-locked, started to kick and plunge, no power on earth could save them.

Even in that moment he did not forget he had to maneuver his own wagon exactly into place at the precise instant that the other came up with it. His rear wheel had to interpose its hub to block the hub of Moon's front wheel, and lock.

Ore jarred, loose chunks spilling off as the wagons hit. The grinding shock seemed to jar the mountain.

The voices of their drivers, the steady hands on the reins, reassured the horses, keeping them from panic. Like the men, they sensed their peril and the need to hold steady.

King had no assurance that the brakes on his own wagon could endure the double strain and check the runaway, even if all else remained under control. Sliding wheels shrieked a protest, but the movement was almost checked.

Almost, but not quite. Steel-shod wheels on a glare of ice could find no bite. They were commencing to slew— a slow, desperate movement outward. And there was no room in which to slide.

"Hold steady!" It was Hard-Rock Baker's voice, as he saw the danger. The miners had stopped just below the teams, clustered like sheep. Now Hard-Rock was leading the way, coming uphill at a run past the horses on the outside, in a cat-like dash on the brink of disaster. The others followed, reached the wagon, braced and shoved hard. If it went off, not one of them would stand a chance.

Silence came down, in which the heavy breathing of men and horses was the only sound. The shuddering movement of wheels stopped. Hard-Rock looked up. His eyes met King's, and a strained grin relaxed his face, but he still held hard against the wagon.

"You boys at the end, get rocks and block the wheels!" he instructed.

They waited while it was done; then Moon lifted a sleeve and swiped it across his face.

"Whoosh!" he gasped. "You darned fool," he added, almost in a whisper. "You goldarned, reckless fool, King! And all these other boys!"

"Nothing like having friends," King said. "Next time you get in a hurry, Em, take a sleigh ride. Now we better get the ore shoved off your wagon."

That was done, and King edged his own wagon ahead and around the bend, then came back. A look at the broken brake rod was enough to show the cause of the near-accident. It had been cut almost in two with a hacksaw; then ashes had been smeared over the cut to make it practically invisible.

"Looks like your hunch was workin' overtime," King sighed. "I'm obliged, Moon."

"So'm I," Moon agreed. "Now I stop to think, I'm too young to die—that way." He shivered as he glanced over the side, then turned, scowling, as Yount came along the road. "What do *you* know about this?" Moon demanded.

Yount had already learned the details from Hard-Rock. He did not immediately reply. Instead, at the bend, he stared down to where a man stood peering up from just below King's team. His attitude was furtive.

"Ask him," Yount suggested. "Even a snooper has no good reason to be here right now—unless he's mighty interested!"

The others turned to look. DeQuille tried to return their glances indifferently, but his own fell. He turned suddenly and started down the road. Almost at once, panic spurring him, he began to run. His feet slipped, and he went tumbling and sliding toward another drop-off. A high cry of terror came dribbling back, and the men turned their heads away.

"He had it coming—but I wouldn't wish that, even for him," Yount said bitterly. "I've been a fool, King," he added, "but I've finally had my eyes opened. I know now who's been two-timing me. Maybe you figured it out before I did."

There was sympathy in King's eyes.

"I think I know what you mean," he agreed.

"He'll be up above," Yount went on. "You won't have to worry about him any more, King. I'll look after him for you as well as myself—he's my meat." Yount turned to the horse he had ridden, swung to the saddle and looked back. "Good luck," he added gruffly.

Yount stopped briefly at his own house after coming down from the mountain. He was bruised and disheveled, and the news had preceded him. Men turned to look at him with new respect in their eyes, not unmixed with pity. At least he'd settled accounts.

Aware of their pity, he was disdainful of it. A look showed him that Wilma had been there and had packed hastily. The stage would be pulling out in a matter of minutes.

He stood looking about the empty rooms, feeling a similar emptiness within himself. She was frightened, and running. It might be better to let her go. And yet, in the end, she had no one besides himself, and for him, there would never be anyone but her. Yount went out, not bothering to close the door. He swung aboard the coach as the driver was settling himself on the box. . . .

Vicki brought the news to King, relaying it soberly.

"Wilma wished us both happiness before she went," she added. "I hope she and Yount can find it now."

"I hope so, too," King agreed. Beyond that there was nothing to say. Yount and Wilma were gone. So was Apperson—who, in a sense, had made the mountain—Helltop. In the end, it had unmade him.

As they turned in at the boarding house, Maggie met them.

"Mr. Van Cleeve has been asking for you, King," she said. "He's quite a lot better, but something seems to worry him."

Van Cleeve was propped up in bed, unquestionably improved. His manner, as when they had met before, was quiet.

"I've been wanting to thank you, Coleman," he said. "I wouldn't be here if it wasn't for you."

King smiled and gripped the tentatively extended hand.

"That's all right," he said. "*I* wouldn't be here, either, but for you."

Van Cleeve nodded thoughtfully. He knew the origin

of that sudden stretch of ice on the road, and whom it had been intended to destroy.

"I'm still in your debt," he insisted, "and I want to do what I can to square myself. Maybe you've wondered why I was in such a hurry to get to Silverhill that day. I was coming to report to Apperson. You see, I falsified the report I gave you."

"Did you, now?" asked King.

"Yes. It was correct in one sense—there was no silver to amount to anything in those specimens you brought me. It appears that the silver must run in a nearly separate vein in the rock. But there was something else—something which I hadn't encountered before, and which Apperson appears to have overlooked entirely. That waste of which he complained so bitterly, as being in the way and hampering operations—apparently there's a great deal of it. And it's copper. My guess is that it will turn out to be many times as valuable as the silver."

King did not tell him that he had guessed that when looking over the dump, and had confirmed it in the assay office after Van Cleeve had so hastily departed. But it was nice to have his own findings confirmed.

"Now that's mighty good news," he declared. "And I sure appreciate your telling me. Right now, I want to relay it to the owner."

Moon and Maggie were in the dining room, along

with Vicki. King told them what Van Cleeve had told him.

"Looks like bonanza instead of *borrasco* for this camp from now on," he added. "Your dad sure made a discovery when he climbed this hill, Vicki."

Her eyes shone, but she seemed only casually interested in the news he had brought.

"So did I when I came out here," Vicki asserted. "And I'll stack mine up against his any day!"